Edit to Death

A Myrtle Clover Cozy Mystery, Volume 14

Elizabeth Spann Craig

Published by Elizabeth Spann Craig, 2019.

This is a work of fiction. Similarities to real people, places, or events are entirely coincidental.

EDIT TO DEATH

First edition. April 2, 2019.

Written by Elizabeth Spann Craig.

For Riley and Elizabeth Ruth

Chapter One

"Did you bring the stuff?" asked Myrtle briskly as she answered her front door.

Miles followed her inside. "You're making it sound like a drug deal. But yes, I brought them."

He laid down a page of cat food coupons on her coffee table. "I think you'll find they're all in order."

"Excellent. I tell you Miles, Pasha is eating me out of house and home," said Myrtle. Pasha was a beautiful, feral, black cat who enjoyed spending time, on a limited basis, with Myrtle.

Miles, always one to keep a careful eye on Pasha's whereabouts asked, "Speaking of, is she around?" He sat down on Myrtle's sofa and she sat in her favorite armchair.

"Currently? No. But by my estimate, she should be jumping through the kitchen window in the next fifteen minutes," said Myrtle.

Miles nodded as if indicating that he now understood the parameters of his visit length. "Shouldn't you be taking the cat to the vet? Aren't owners supposed to report unusual changes in activity and appetite?"

Myrtle said, "Pasha couldn't be healthier. Her coat and eyes shine. Her teeth are tartar-free. The problem is that Pasha is too good at hunting. She has been out there, outside, relentlessly subduing nature for quite some time and now has eliminated her prey. There's very little for the poor dear to catch now."

Miles, who had seen evidence of Pasha's successful hunting expeditions, shifted uneasily on the sofa. "There was certainly a fairly regular display of Pasha's trophies. Bats, snakes, chipmunks, birds, lizards, shrews, and other assorted small creatures."

"She's a brilliant hunter," said Myrtle proudly. "It's just that her exceptional prowess is now creating issues. Anyway, that's why she's been hungrier than usual. I haven't seen any little corpses scattered around and she's been asking for canned food. That seems a direct connection to me. Thus, the coupons from the newspaper. And I've already procured Red and Elaine's coupons, too."

Miles nodded. "I foresee the next step is a trip to the grocery store to stock up."

"Well, if I time the coupons with an upcoming sale, Pasha will be sitting pretty for a while," said Myrtle. "And the sale starts tomorrow."

Miles raised his eyebrows. "That is a remarkable thing to know. The flyers for the sales don't distribute until Wednesday morning. How do you know not to stock up now?"

Myrtle gave him a smug look. "I taught the manager of the store. Sometimes he gives me tips. He has to know what's going to be on sale so that he can arrange for the staff to put sale items on the end caps."

Miles nodded. This was no real surprise to him. Myrtle had taught English to nearly everyone in town over a certain age.

His eye lingered on a stack of papers on Myrtle's table. "Speaking of teaching, why does it look like you're grading papers? You have a red pen out. I'm having some horrible flashbacks."

Myrtle shot the papers a look of disgust. "That's because I'm basically grading papers. Sloan has gone off the deep end and the paper's editing was non-existent. You must have noticed."

"No matter how much I'd have noticed, it wouldn't have been on the scale of how much *you* noticed," said Miles. "Why has Sloan gone off the deep end?"

Sloan Jones was the editor of the *Bradley Bugle* and another former student of Myrtle's. He was also her editor since she wrote a helpful hints column . . . and, when circumstances allowed, covered crime.

"I thought you'd have heard. Sally broke up with him. He's devastated and completely preoccupied with moping around over Sally—to the extent that the paper has 'there, their, and they're' errors, among other grievous problems," clucked Myrtle.

Miles nodded. "And you persuaded Sloan to send the stories your way before he ran them in the paper."

"Naturally! I couldn't have my name associated with the paper in its current iteration. I have a position to uphold in town. He emails them to me, and then I print them out so that I can pull out my red pen. I don't seem to edit as well with a digital copy. After I input the changes digitally, then I send them back to him. He's incredibly grateful," said Myrtle firmly.

Miles was less certain.

"Don't you want a break? Those papers are fairly bleeding red ink."

"And they should be! Take a look," said Myrtle, motioning to the pile of papers as if it needed to be handled with gloves.

Miles carefully picked them up and sifted through them to keep them in order. "You've gotten carried away."

"Carried away? With good grammar in the newspaper?" said Myrtle, looking at Miles as if he'd lost his mind.

"Some of this stuff needs to be corrected. I doubt Sloan intended for the possessive *its* here, for sure. But you're correcting subjunctive stuff, too. Let's put it this way, Myrtle. If Sloan is as low as you're saying, he might cry when he gets this. You don't want to be responsible for that, do you?"

Myrtle flinched. If there was one thing she hated, it was tears. "Well, I suppose it's easy for me to get on a roll. It's hard to see the stories littered with mistakes and not do anything about them."

"I'd recommend restraint. If we head to the diner for lunch, you might be able to overlook at least some of the more minute transgressions. I'd think it would be very dispiriting for a newspaper editor to get revisions like that. Particularly if Sloan is already as upset as you say," said Miles.

"All right then, distract me."

Miles knit his brows.

Myrtle sighed. "Distract me from what I'm doing. Be entertaining. Tell me what's going on with you."

Miles looked pleased. He reached into the pocket of his slacks and pulled out a new phone. "*This* is what's going on with me."

"A phone?" asked Myrtle. Her gaze strayed back to the red pen and paper.

"Yes, but it's a *new* phone. It has all sorts of bells and whistles," said Miles eagerly.

Myrtle sighed. "All right, I'll bite. Why not show me one of the bells or whistles?"

Miles stooped next to her. "See this icon on the home screen? It's a voice recorder. It's excellent. The recordings are clear even if the person speaking isn't talking directly into the phone."

Myrtle lifted an eyebrow. "And what are you doing with this voice recorder? Anything nefarious? Or at least interesting?"

"I'm recording my doctor visits," said Miles proudly.

Myrtle nodded, glancing at the red pen again.

"You see, when I'm sitting there in a gown and the doctor is giving all sorts of information and instructions, I can't pay enough attention to take it all in. All I'm thinking about is the fact that I'm sitting in a gown and how ridiculous I appear." He looked down gratefully at his current attire of khaki pants and a blue button-down shirt. "Now I can listen to his instructions whenever I want." To prove it, he hit the icon and the doctor's voice droned on the importance of eating bananas.

Myrtle perked up. "Bananas sound good right now. Actually, food in general sounds good. So we'll go to Bo's Diner? I hear that they have a new menu item there."

Miles put a hand to his chest. "Careful, Myrtle. I'm not prepared for shocks like that. That menu hasn't changed since the 1950s, has it?"

"It's the grandson. He's wanting to make things a little more modern up there. Apparently, he's even putting the diner up on social media," said Myrtle. "He's taking some sort of poll to see if folks are willing to try something new at the diner—and then diners are supposed to vote on what their favorite new menu item is."

"I'm scared to ask," said Miles.

"It's nothing healthy, so it probably won't appeal to you. It's a pimento cheese dog with barbeque sauce."

Miles made a face. "I'll plan on sticking with some tried-and true-offerings."

"Well, let's head on out, if we're going to make it back in time for our soap opera," said Myrtle, standing up.

Miles flinched a bit at the words *our soap opera*. "Really, Myrtle . . ." But he was cut off by the doorbell.

Myrtle frowned. "For heaven's sake. Don't tell me we're doing this again. I don't want another record day of people dropping by to say hi." She strode toward the door, cane in hand in a somewhat aggressive posture.

Miles said mildly, "Everyone was simply being nice. Checking up on you."

"I suspect Red planted some sort of horrid rumor that I was under the weather, just so people would come visit me and tie up my day." Myrtle peered out the window. "Pearl Epps!"

It wasn't clear from Myrtle's voice whether she was happy to see Pearl at her door or not, but she did open it.

Pearl beamed at her. She was a tall, thin woman of about seventy-five. She was always carefully made-up with lots of brightly colored cosmetics and wouldn't have left the house unless she was dressed up. Today's outfit was a floral dress with blue ruffles covering the top. She carried a large tote bag.

"Myrtle!" she said, reaching out to give Myrtle a hug.

Myrtle hugged her briefly before pulling back and gesturing into her living room. "Please come in, Pearl. You know Miles, don't you?"

Pearl beamed at him. "I do, yes. Oh goodness, I'm not interrupting anything, am I? Lunch plans?"

Miles exchanged a look with Myrtle. "Nothing that can't be put off."

Pearl grinned. "You *did* have lunch plans until the doorbell rang. Well now I feel like a genius."

Myrtle smiled politely.

Pearl lifted the tote bag onto the small dining room table and carefully unloaded a plastic container. "Lunch! Or supper, if you like. It's chicken, broccoli, and rice."

Myrtle said in a suspicious voice, "Has Red been talking about me? I swear he's told everyone that I'm laid up in bed or something. People *keep* coming over . . . although you're the first to bring food."

Pearl gave a trilling laugh. "If he has, I haven't heard about it. What a horrible thing for him to do."

Myrtle said, "A *typical* thing for him to do. If he hasn't, then what is all of this delicious food in aid of, Pearl?"

Pearl beamed at her. "I have a favor to ask of you."

Myrtle nodded, unsurprised. "Which is?"

Pearl hesitated as her gaze fell on the stack of papers. "What on earth is that?"

Miles said, "Myrtle has gotten carried away with editing the local newspaper."

"I thought maybe a red pen had leaked out," said Pearl slowly.

Myrtle asked, "The favor, Pearl?"

Pearl sighed. "Well, now I'm feeling a little anxious about it, but the truth is that I was going to ask you to edit my memoir. I was hoping that maybe you wouldn't be too busy to take it on, but I didn't know that you were editing the entire newspaper. Which, actually, looks like it might be a time-consuming job." Again, her gaze slowly tracked over the stack of papers and the angry-looking red marks covering the one on the top.

Myrtle shrugged. "I don't have an *official* role in editing the newspaper, although Sloan should certainly put my name on the masthead, now that I think about it. It's just that he's too distracted right now to do a good job."

Pearl raised her eyebrows. "Because of Sally dumping him."

Miles winced. He was always surprised how everyone knew everyone else's business in small towns.

"Exactly. But I could scale back what I'm doing. In fact, Miles inferred that it might be wise to scale it back anyway," said Myrtle. "That I was being rather harsh."

Pearl looked more hopeful. "That would be wonderful, Myrtle. And yes, I brought the food to butter you up. I know you're fantastic at proofreading. I can't really pay you very much, but I can feed you."

"Could I see the manuscript?" asked Myrtle.

Pearl eagerly reached into the tote bag again. "I'd hoped you'd say that. I brought it along just in case."

Myrtle took a large bundle of papers from Pearl. She had tied a ribbon around them. Myrtle warily skimmed the first twenty pages or so to estimate the time commitment it would take. The pages were fairly clear of mistakes.

"I'll do it," said Myrtle.

Pearl clapped her hands. "Oh, wonderful! You've made my day."

Miles said, "What made you decide to write a memoir?"

Pearl turned her bright blue eyes his way. "It sounds crazy, doesn't it? I used to think that memoirs were written by people with exciting and extraordinary lives. People who traveled and moved in interesting circles and lived through historic times. But then I started reading a lot of memoirs at the library and realized that the most interesting ones of all were the ones that hit closer to home."

Miles said politely, "I'm sure it will be very interesting. You'll focus on your family?"

There was a shadow that passed in front of Pearl's eyes and she gave a short laugh. "You could say that." She paused. "I may be giving the wrong impression about this memoir, actually. Or, maybe I'm letting you make assumptions about the type of book that I'd write."

Miles reddened a little as if he'd been caught out making exactly those sorts of assumptions about the old lady in the floral dress with the ruffles. But Myrtle gazed thoughtfully at Pearl.

"You mean that this isn't just a sweet tale about how your grandmother worked alongside your grandfather in the fields? And how your father picked himself up by his bootstraps to make something of his life? And so on?" asked Myrtle.

Pearl smiled at her, but this time the smile didn't seem to reach up to her blue eyes. "It's not that kind of story. I'm not trying to be deliberately mysterious, really."

Myrtle said, "Well, you're certainly supplying a teaser, aren't you?"

Pearl twinkled at her. "Just to ensure that you'll dive right in. But I think you'll find the story surprising. What's that new genre they talk about? Domestic noir?"

Chapter Two

Myrtle gave her a thoughtful look. "If you've written domestic noir, I'll be checking out your book immediately after lunch."

Miles said in a hesitant voice, "Pearl, I'm just curious. What made you write a memoir? Just that you'd been reading them and decided to try your hand at them? Or was it something else?"

A cloud passed over Pearl's face. She said, "A very good question. The answer is that secrets are totally destroying our family. Especially my relationship with my sister. I don't feel as if I can even look her in the eye anymore, and she has no idea. You know what a virtuous woman Nell is. I want to clear the air and prevent any more damage. I felt like a book would be the best way of exposing the secrets because I could include details and explanations. Maybe, in a way, excuses. I've titled the book *Secrets*. I'm ready to put it all out there and let the chips fall where they may."

Miles cleared his throat. "And your family? What do they think of your doing that?" He had an uneasy look on his face as if he knew what *he* would think about that, if something like that happened in his family.

Pearl pressed her lips together and then said, "They aren't real excited over it. But they haven't thought it through like me. If they had, they'd know that this is the only way for our family to move forward and heal. For justice, in a way. The family had no idea that I was even finished with it."

"They haven't kept up with your progress?" asked Myrtle.

Pearl chuckled, but it wasn't really a happy sound. "Not at all. They just thought that I was planning on writing a book, but that it would never really happen. Or that I'd start out and maybe get a couple of chapters in and then I'd give up on it or get busy or something. No, they were very surprised. I'm not sure what they thought I was doing on my laptop, but they obviously didn't think I was working on a book. Maybe they thought my clunky dinosaur of a laptop didn't even have the memory for a book. They have considered the thing as just a paperweight ever since I covered the outside with stickers. You know how much I like decorating things."

Miles said, "What happened when you told them you were finished?"

"I had the whole family over for supper last night and announced that the book was done and that I was moving on to the next step today—which was having you edit it." She blushed a little. "At least, I hoped to convince you."

Myrtle gave her a wry look. "You were apparently pretty confident that you could."

Pearl watched as Myrtle sifted through the papers some more. She looked uncomfortable. "Maybe you could take a look at it after I'm gone. It makes me feel anxious having an editor read it while I'm right here."

"I don't even have my red pen in hand," said Myrtle, raising her eyebrows. Then she frowned. "Now Pearl, are you going to be really sensitive when I make suggestions and things? Should I be careful with what I tell you?"

"Oh no! No, I want the truth and I want the thing corrected." She hesitated. "I know I printed it out so it would be easier for you to edit, but *is* it easier that way? Or should I have just emailed you a copy of it or something?"

"No, this is fine. I was just telling Miles that I edit better on paper," said Myrtle. "All right. I'm not sure how long it's going to take me to do it, but I should get an idea twenty or thirty pages into it."

"That's perfect. I feel so much better now that it's in your hands. And I'll leave you both to your lunch," said Pearl, standing up.

Myrtle said, "What you've brought me is worthy of supper. Miles and I are going out to grab lunch and then tonight I won't have to cook because of the lovely casserole you brought. It's the perfect day."

Pearl smiled at her and then hesitated. "I might check in with you later. Just see what your first impressions are."

"Of course. I'm not sure how far in I'll be," said Myrtle. She was starting to wonder if Pearl was going to be one of those who liked to hover.

"Right. Okay, well, thanks again."

She left and Myrtle said to Miles, "Let's head over to Bo's Diner before any more people come in. Just let me stick this in the fridge."

They were walking to the front door when Pasha's face appeared in the front window. "Hungry again," said Myrtle, shaking her head.

"Can't she wait until we get back? We won't be very long if we're going to come back in time for *Tomorrow's Promise*," said Miles.

"I'll just open the window in the front and the back one in the kitchen. Thank goodness it hasn't been buggy outside this year. I've had to pop the screens off half my windows to allow Pasha egress," said Myrtle.

Bo's Diner was thankfully not as crowded as it usually was. And it was only minutes until they'd received their food.

Miles cast a wary eye on Myrtle's pimento cheese dog with barbeque sauce. "What does that odd concoction taste like?"

Myrtle took a thoughtful bite. "Actually, it's delicious. Bacon, tomato, pimento cheese, barbeque sauce, hot dog—what's not to like?"

Miles shuddered. "It would end up chasing me all night long when I was trying to sleep."

"Only because you have a very delicate digestive system," said Myrtle. "You certainly won't have to worry about your salad chasing you around. That's a very mild-mannered menu item and the toppings look particularly wimpy today."

Miles said, "We can't all have cast-iron stomachs. On other topics, what did you make of Pearl? Didn't you think that was a sort of weird conversation?"

Myrtle said, "It *was* weird. First off, I never would have seen Pearl Prentiss Epps writing a memoir of any kind. I mean, she's sharp as a tack, but I don't picture her as being introspective enough to write her life story. Secondly, I'd have imagined that any memoir that Pearl wrote would be something about her family tree—the story of her family a couple of generations ago, and then her upbringing."

Miles nodded. "Like you mentioned—her family had come from nothing, and through hard work had made themselves a good life in Bradley."

"Precisely. But this seemed like a completely different project. She wasn't nearly as relaxed as she had made out," said Myrtle.

Miles thought about this. "She seemed relaxed to me. To me, it just seemed like the whole thing was very orchestrated: bringing the food and the manuscript in the tote bag, etc. She certainly was determined to have you help her out."

"Determined and ill at ease. Pearl wanted to get a reaction from me right away, remember? And she might have been smiling, but underneath that, she seemed very tense."

"*Did* you have a first impression of the memoir?" asked Miles.

Myrtle shrugged. "I only glanced through it to make sure that there weren't a lot of egregious errors on every page. If there had been, I'd have had to ask for more money and more time."

"You didn't ask for *any* money," said Miles.

"Yes, but that's because she's definitely going to give me *something*. It won't be enough for editing an entire book, but it won't be nothing. I know Pearl—she'll make it right," said Myrtle.

Miles said, "At any rate, Red will be pleased. That looked like a huge manuscript. It should keep you busy and out of trouble."

Myrtle said, "Red has been so busy that he's not even paying any attention to what I'm doing. Aside from sending people over to harass me."

Miles raised his eyebrows. "That's a change. Ordinarily, he's on top of whatever you're up to."

"Oh, Jack's been especially active. He's such a brilliant little boy, you know."

"I know," said Miles quickly, as if hoping to head off Myrtle from cataloging Jack's many areas of genius.

"He has a mind like a steel trap," said Myrtle proudly. "He figured out how to work the locks on the door and Red had to get deadbolts put in so they could keep Jack in the house. Jack would push the stool over to the door, fiddle with the locks, and let himself out. He came over here twice, the little dear."

"I bet that *has* kept Red busy," said Miles.

"And Elaine has been keeping him on his toes, too," said Myrtle.

"She's not trying that healthy cooking hobby again, is she?" asked Miles with a shudder. "I *like* healthy food and what she was preparing even scared me."

"No, she's moved on to another hobby. Photography," said Myrtle.

"Hasn't she tried photography before?" asked Miles, crinkling his forehead.

"Yes, but she's trying it again. She felt badly because she had all of this expensive photographic equipment and then abandoned the hobby," said Myrtle. "Sloan is keeping her busy taking pictures for the newspaper. Sometimes, she takes Jack along with her."

Miles said, "What kind of photojournalism assignments is Sloan sending her on?"

"I suspect that Sloan is just trying to keep her busy as a favor to Red. Unfortunately, Elaine isn't the best photographer ever. She took photos at Gemma Cook's 100th birthday. I suppose a handful were okay," said Myrtle in an unconvinced voice.

Miles said, "Well, it's hard to look one's best when one is turning 100. Perhaps the fault doesn't lie all on Elaine's side."

"It would have helped things if Elaine's thumb hadn't appeared in most of the pictures," said Myrtle.

"Ah."

Myrtle said, "Anyway, that's the kind of stuff Sloan is sending her on. So the fact of the matter is that Red has been very busy *and* Elaine has been very busy. You've been rather busy, yourself, experimenting with your phone and whatnot."

Miles said, "Why do I have the feeling a big statement is about to follow?"

Myrtle said sternly, "Because I haven't had very many opportunities to get rides from any of you. I have been walking into town so much that I feel as if I've been training for a marathon."

"Do they *have* walking marathons?" mused Miles.

"That's why I'll be talking with Boone Epps about used cars," said Myrtle in a satisfied voice.

Miles stared at her. "But you haven't had a car in ages. Not since I've moved here."

"Exactly. I didn't need one, either. But now I'd like the convenience of being able to hop into a car and drive somewhere without asking someone for a ride. Someone who's too busy to give me one," said Myrtle.

Miles said, "Well, if you wanted to get Red's attention, I'm sure this will be the way to do it. I doubt he wants you driving around."

"That's because he's ageist. I'm the safest driver in Bradley," said Myrtle.

"Because you drive twenty miles an hour," said Miles.

"There's no reason to rush," sniffed Myrtle.

They finished their meals and spoke to a few people on the way out. Then Miles drove back to Myrtle's house.

Myrtle unlocked the door and Miles walked over to pick up the remote. "Just in time for the show," he said.

Myrtle nodded absently. She stared at the table. "Where is Pearl's manuscript?"

"The manuscript? You put it on the table." Miles turned on the television and the dramatic theme music for *Tomorrow's Promise* blared.

"Mute that thing," grouched Myrtle.

"The show?" Miles frowned at her. "Wasn't it the whole reason we didn't order pie at Bo's Diner?"

Myrtle glared at him and Miles muted the show.

Myrtle said, "Did you move it?"

"Move what? The manuscript? I didn't even touch the thing," said Miles.

Myrtle stood in the living room and slowly turned to see every corner of the small room.

Miles said, "Maybe you wandered into the kitchen with it." Now he stood up and walked over to Myrtle, staring at the spot on the table where the manuscript should have been.

"Miles, the only time I went into the kitchen, I was putting Pearl's food into the fridge. I wouldn't have lugged a seven- or eight-pound manuscript into the kitchen with me," said Myrtle.

They stared at each other.

"Your windows are all open," said Miles slowly.

Myrtle frowned. "Do you think that maybe Pearl had second thoughts about having me look at it, after all? That maybe she started considering the impact her memoir might have on her family?"

Miles shook his head. "No way. She was clearly sold on the idea of putting family secrets out there. She even thought that the book would *solve* problems by forcing them out in the open."

Myrtle nodded. "Besides, Pearl would just call me and tell me she'd changed her mind. She wouldn't break into my house and take the thing. Seriously. A seventy-something year-old woman climbing through my windows?"

Miles said, "But she apparently told her family last night that she was taking the manuscript to the next stop on its publication journey—editing."

Myrtle fumbled for her phone. "I'm calling Pearl."

She found the number in her contacts, dialed it, and waited. "She's not answering."

Miles said in a reasonable voice, "Pearl could just have her ringer turned off. Maybe she's at a church meeting. Or eating lunch. We can't leap to the conclusion that something is wrong."

"I'm leaping," said Myrtle grimly. "Pearl loves that phone of hers and I've never called her when she didn't pick it right up. She'd even answer a call in the middle of Thanksgiving dinner. We're going straight over to her house this minute. And while we're there, we're going to ask her family where that manuscript is."

A few minutes later, Miles pulled the car up to the curb in front of Pearl's house. It was a beautiful gray brick house with climbing roses clinging to the walls and a riot of flowers and flowering shrubs in the front yard instead of grass.

Miles said, "I've always thought this kind of front garden made a lot of sense. No lawn to mow and it looks pretty most of the year."

Myrtle said, "Pearl and Hubert are always out here messing with it, though—weeding it, spraying it, deadheading old blossoms. It's not exactly low-maintenance. Plus, Dusty would flip his lid."

Dusty was Myrtle's yardman. He was lazy to the bone and would do anything to avoid mowing her grass. In Dusty's opinion, it was always either too hot, too wet, or too dry to mow. But his fee was reasonable and never increased. Plus, he would use a weed-trimmer around Myrtle's gnomes whenever Myrtle was annoyed enough at Red to drag them out into the front yard.

Myrtle walked carefully down Pearl's cobblestone front walk to the front door, leaning on her cane to ensure that she didn't stumble. "Treacherous," she muttered.

She rang the doorbell and then rapped on the front door without waiting for anyone to respond to the bell. Myrtle tapped her foot impatiently.

"Maybe Pearl went out to lunch," said Miles mildly.

"Without Hubert? His car is out front."

"Maybe it was a girls' lunch," he suggested.

Myrtle just tightened her lips and rapped on the door again.

A second later, Hubert, Pearl's husband, answered the door. He gazed at Myrtle wordlessly. Hubert was a big fellow with a barrel chest and long out-of-fashion sideburns.

Myrtle and Hubert stared at each other. Myrtle waited for a greeting or at least words of some sort and Hubert seemed to be waiting to try to find any words at all.

Myrtle opened her mouth to speak, but snapped it back shut again as Hubert finally started croaking out some words.

"Dead. She's dead," he said, eyes open wide.

Chapter Three

Myrtle gave Hubert a sharp look. "Have you called Red?" He still gazed blankly at her.

"Have you called the police?" she snapped. "Or an ambulance? Maybe you just think she's dead."

Hubert's expression didn't change and Myrtle gave an impatient sigh. "Miles, could you call Red?"

Miles was already dialing his number.

Myrtle said briskly, "All right, Hubert. Why don't you take a seat?" She pointed to a white wicker chair on the front porch and Hubert obediently headed over to it and plopped down.

Then Myrtle took out a tissue from her purse and carefully pushed the front door open. She didn't see anything. Myrtle walked through the small entranceway into the den and then to the staircase against the back wall.

There she saw Pearl, her head in a very odd position on the floor. The rest of Pearl was on the stairs behind her. Pearl's eyes were staring blankly in an expression that mimicked Hubert's, except blanker.

"Do we need an ambulance?" called Miles from the porch.

"I'm afraid not," said Myrtle grimly. "But we will need Red."

"He's not picking up, so I called the station and the deputy is coming over," said Miles.

Myrtle muttered, "That's right; he was supposed to be speaking at some sort of community policing seminar."

"Which deputy is this, now?" asked Miles.

"A new one. The last one thought Bradley was a little too small for him," said Myrtle.

"What is this guy like?" asked Miles.

"Not as bright as the last one," said Myrtle. "And he requires a bit of hand-holding."

Miles gave every indication of being about to ask her another question and she quickly interjected, "Can you keep an eye on Hubert? I'll be right back."

She crouched down to see if there were any clues that she could see near Pearl without touching or moving her. She couldn't see any broken fingernails or any other signs of a struggle. It didn't look as if she'd been strangled and then shoved down the stairs. There were no rugs on the stairs that might have tripped her up. Under the circumstances, and judging from what had happened with the manuscript, her fall and death seemed extremely suspicious.

Myrtle carefully walked into the den and glanced around. There were no signs of a manuscript anywhere. She looked for a chunky, clunky computer with stickers on it and didn't see one. She walked to the kitchen. Again, no sign of any stack of papers and no computer.

Myrtle walked, frowning, back out to the porch. She was relieved to see that Hubert seemed to be himself again.

"I'm so sorry about Pearl," said Myrtle to Hubert.

He nodded and gave a big sigh. "It was a shock to see her like that. I'd left for the grocery store to stock up on beer and came back home with it. Then I remembered I had a prescription to pick up at the drugstore, so I headed over there."

Myrtle said, "Did you speak with Pearl when you came back from the grocery store?"

Hubert said roughly, "I didn't see her, and she didn't call out to me, if that's what you mean. But I was nowhere near the staircase, so I couldn't see her—if she was already there. I only went to the kitchen and then I was back in the car again."

Myrtle said slowly, "Did you know that Pearl came to visit me, today?"

Hubert shrugged. "She mentioned something about it last night, but I didn't realize that's where she was off to this morning."

"But you knew that she had written a memoir?" asked Myrtle.

"A book?" Hubert shrugged dismissively again. "She yakked about all kinds of things, you know. Sometimes I'd listen, sometimes not. Yeah, she'd mentioned that she'd written a book. But I had no real interest in it. I haven't read a book since I was in school."

A police car pulled into Hubert's driveway.

Myrtle frowned. "I thought the deputy was coming. That's Red."

Her son had inherited her height and was over six feet tall. The red hair that had given him his nickname was now turning gray—something he tended to blame his mother for.

He narrowed his eyes at Myrtle and went directly to Hubert. "You okay, Hubert?" he asked, leaning over to look him in the eyes as he sat in the wicker chair.

Hubert said in a broken voice, "She's dead."

"I'm sorry. You just stay right here and we're going to sort it all out," said Red in a grim voice.

He strode into the house after nodding in greeting to Miles. Two minutes later, he walked back out again looking even grimmer.

"Hubert, may I speak with you for a few minutes? Let's talk in your yard over on that bench, if that's all right," said Red.

Myrtle and Miles watched as Red and Hubert engaged in a relatively short conversation.

Miles said, "I could tell you weren't very fond of Hubert," said Miles.

"He gave Pearl nothing but grief while she was alive. The thought that he might have killed someone I consider a friend is *very, very* vexing!" said Myrtle.

Miles said, "He does seem very affected by Pearl's death."

"He's probably wondering who's going to feed him and wash his clothes now that she's gone," said Myrtle uncharitably.

"Red's motioning us over," said Miles.

"Makes more sense to speak with us here and leave Hubert over there," said Myrtle. Which is what Red ended up doing.

Red strolled up to them and plopped down in a chair on the front porch. "Mama, I hope you have an excellent explanation as to how you're involved with yet another dead body."

"I'm involved with this one because she's *not* just a dead body. I'm surprised at you, Red! This is Pearl Prentiss Epps. She taught you Sunday school and knew you since you were a little guy." Myrtle glared at her son.

Red sighed. "I know that, Mama. I'm just trying to mentally distance myself from that fact. It's tough to see her like that. But I have the state police on the way and they'll be able to tell me if Pearl had a coronary event that prefaced her fall. Maybe she had a stroke and fell. At least I know that she couldn't have been there for long."

Myrtle gave him a hard look. "What the state police will find is that Pearl was likely *shoved* down the stairs. And I think that's what you're going to conclude, too, once you hear what I have to say."

Red groaned. "I was afraid you would say there was some sort of story behind this."

Miles cleared his throat. "I can confirm it."

Red nodded. "Okay, that makes me feel better. Go ahead and fill me in."

Myrtle did, finishing with, "And when we came back in from Bo's Diner, the manuscript had disappeared."

Red frowned. "So you're alleging that someone broke into your house and stole Pearl's book?"

"I'm not *alleging* it. I'm stating it. The manuscript is gone. I hardly think that the cat picked it up and spirited it away," said Myrtle in an exasperated voice.

"Could you simply have put it somewhere and just thought that you had left it in the living room?" asked Red. He sounded hopeful.

Miles shook his head. "Sorry, Red. She left it in the living room and that's that. And all the windows were open for the cat to come and go as she pleased. It seems that someone took advantage of that fact to climb in."

"Directly across the street from the police chief? And in sight of an extremely nosy neighbor by the name of Erma Sherman?" Red knit his eyebrows.

"A police chief who's so busy that he's rarely home. And Erma has been laid up with some malady that I'd rather not know about," said Myrtle.

"And which Erma is likely to fill us in on later," said Miles glumly.

"Besides," added Myrtle, "I had a window open facing the *back* yard, too. Someone could have easily slipped back there and climbed in."

"I don't know about *easily*," said Red, frowning. "People aren't quite as nimble as Pasha is. But let's just say that it's possible. *Why* would somebody do such a thing? I think about Pearl Prentiss and all that comes to mind is a sweet little old lady with an unremarkable life."

Myrtle nodded. "That's exactly the problem. That's what came to mind for me, too. But Pearl indicated that she was tired of keeping secrets. Perhaps her family wasn't as tired of it and wanted to stop her. Because soon it would be all over town that Pearl and her family weren't as sweet and unremarkable as they seemed. And I just can't see Pearl *falling* down the stairs. It's simply too coincidental that Pearl would suffer a fatal fall down the stairs at the same time that her memoir is stolen from my house. Besides, Pearl was a coordinated woman—she could do marvelous needlework. And she was holding nothing in her hands as she went down the stairs. There was no rug there to trip over."

Red nodded. "All right. While I'm inside, I'll be sure to look for copies of this book." He paused. "I don't suppose she wrote the thing in longhand, did she?"

"No, she typed it on her computer and printed it out. But when I was inside, I didn't see her computer or any other copies of her manuscript," said Myrtle.

Red gave her a hard look. "You didn't go upstairs, I hope."

"And step over poor Pearl? Of course not," said Myrtle.

"Okay. Well, it's possible that we'll find the computer upstairs in her bedroom. I'll keep an eye out for it. Now, if both of you could go ahead and head back home, I'd appreciate it. The state police will be here at any time now." And without another word, Red walked back to Hubert.

Miles drove back while Myrtle sat quietly thinking. "You know, we're going to need to make Pearl's daughter, Rose, a casserole."

Miles gave Myrtle a wary sideways glance. "She doesn't even know about her mother's death. A casserole can be put off until at least tomorrow. And remember, we don't usually have much luck with these 'in sympathy' casseroles. It might be better to pick up something from the store."

"*We*? The casseroles are always my concoctions. You usually won't even allow yourself to be credited in their creation. And everyone knows that homemade is better than something store bought."

Miles's mouth tightened, but he didn't reply.

"You have a point about Rose, though. Let's plan on seeing her first thing tomorrow. In the meantime, we can relax for a little while," said Myrtle.

Miles raised his eyebrows. "Now that's not something I usually hear you say right after a murder has happened."

"Well, finding Pearl has really worn me out. I'm not talking about relaxing the rest of the *day*, just long enough for me to get my bearings. I'll need to write up a story for Sloan, of course, too," said Myrtle.

Miles frowned. "You know that Sloan rarely wants you covering crime stories. Red puts pressure on him to keep you on the helpful hints column."

Myrtle waved her hand in the air dismissively. "Pooh. Sloan is down in the dumps with his breakup, remember? I'm effectively doing all of the editing. That story won't get covered if I don't do it and that would be a pity because it's going to be a big story. Pearl Prentiss is an important person in this town. She's lived here all her life, knows just about everybody in Bradley, and was involved in all sorts of activities here. It would be a travesty if her murder wasn't reported."

Miles said cautiously, "But Myrtle, Red didn't seem convinced that it *was* a murder."

Myrtle snorted. "He'll come around. There's too much evidence to the contrary. Besides, I won't explicitly come out and *say* it's murder."

They both looked over at Myrtle's empty table.

"All right," said Myrtle briskly. "Let's not dwell on sad things right now. On with *Tomorrow's Promise*. I want to find out if Christine will die in that ambulance or if they're going to bring her back for another season. The idea of ending the last show with her struggling for her life in an ambulance! The producers of this soap sure have a lot of nerve."

Fortunately for the producers of the show, Christine did *not* die in the ambulance, although it was all very harrowing for a while. Toward the end of the soap, the plot line became a lot more pedestrian. Myrtle, who was not at all concerned whether Rohan would end up together with Penelope, started writing her piece for Sloan.

At least, she was working on it until her doorbell rang. She raised her eyebrows. "Like I said, Miles, it appears that Red is spreading rumors about the tenuous quality of my health. I'm going to have to put a note on my door, signed by my doctor, to combat this."

She walked over and peered outside, then drew back in surprise. "Rose," she murmured to Miles.

"Pardon?" he asked.

"Rose!" she hissed. "Pearl's daughter."

Chapter Four

Myrtle quickly pulled open the door. "Rose, my dear, I'm just so sorry. Can you come inside?" Then she noticed that Rose had a dog in tow. The dog grinned apologetically at Myrtle as if it knew it shouldn't be there.

"Oh no, I can't—I'd feel bad about bringing Buster in here," said Rose. Her jet-black, shoulder-length hair made the paleness of her complexion look even whiter in comparison. She always had a fragile look about her and she looked especially delicate today with huge shadows under her eyes. Her eyes were red from tears.

Myrtle gave Buster the once-over. Pasha didn't appear to be around, so there would be no conflicts there. "Buster seems fairly well-behaved. We can sit in the kitchen. Please come in."

"Thanks. Buster isn't mine. One of my jobs is being a dog-walker. I fit it in around some of the other stuff I do," said Rose. Her voice sounded hollow as if she were speaking on automatic pilot.

Rose and Buster followed Myrtle in. "You know Miles don't you?"

Rose gave Miles a small smile. "Good to see you, Miles."

Miles nodded and smiled back, following them both into the kitchen.

Myrtle said, "You actually must have read my mind, Rose. Miles and I were planning on visiting you tomorrow morning with a casserole in tow. We're just so sorry about what happened to your poor mother."

Rose's eyes welled up with tears, but to Myrtle's relief, they didn't spill over. She said, "That's so sweet of you."

Miles shifted. Never happy with Myrtle's cooking, the look on his face said that it wasn't a sweet gesture at all.

Rose continued, "You must wonder what I'm doing here, just after hearing about Mother." Her voice trembled a little.

Myrtle shook her head. "Not really, sweetie. I'd imagine you're looking for some sort of explanation or more information. Sometimes men aren't great about giving that out. I'm thinking you didn't hear much from either Red or your father."

Rose shook her head. "Red was, naturally, asking me questions. And my father was just sort of off in a fog. I just want to know what happened." Her voice was tight and tense, and her hands holding Buster's leash were shaking.

Myrtle said, "Can't I get you something to eat? To drink?"

Rose shook her head.

Myrtle sighed and said, "If your mom hadn't come over to see me this morning, I might just have figured it was a terrible tragedy that she fell down the stairs. I still *do* think it's a terrible tragedy, and you know how fond I was of your mother. I'm very much afraid that there must have been foul play involved."

Rose's dark eyes were huge in her pale face. "Murdered! I wondered when Red was asking me all of those questions.

Could it have had something to do with her book? I know that's why she came over to see you this morning."

"I wish I knew. Unfortunately, I didn't have much of a chance to take a look at it before it was stolen while Miles and I were at lunch. But Pearl hinted that it would involve exposing family secrets." Myrtle paused and studied Rose, who had hung her head and was staring at a confused Buster.

After a few moments, Rose said in a small voice, "Yes, Mother hinted something like that to us last night. She was in such an odd mood. On one hand, she seemed energetic and proud that she had completed this book. None of us had any idea that she'd taken it so seriously and that she was actually *working* on it. She'd thrown out the suggestion some time ago that she wanted to write her memoirs and I'm afraid that no one really listened to her or believed that she would do it."

Miles said, "No one saw her typing? Working on it?"

Rose shook her head. "I mean, sometimes I noticed her laptop out, but I never thought anything of it. I figured she was just looking at recipes online or quilt patterns or something like that."

"This laptop," said Myrtle. "When I was in your parents' house a while ago, I didn't see any evidence of it at all. Do you know what happened to it?"

Rose frowned. "It's gone?"

"Well, I suppose it might have been upstairs. I didn't go upstairs, of course. But I made a cursory search for it downstairs and didn't see it. I was specifically looking out for it because of the theft of the manuscript," said Myrtle.

Rose stared at her. "Someone *stole* it?"

Rose swayed a bit unsteadily and Myrtle quickly said, "Here, have a seat."

Miles gave Myrtle a look. Rose had looked as though she might keel over there for a second. And she wore a thinness and fragility that didn't seem healthy.

Myrtle said, "Your mother was such a beloved figure in this town, you know. I'm very sorry that she's gone."

Rose said, "I can't imagine who could do such a thing. Such an awful thing." As she was saying it, a flush rose up from her neck and covered her face in splotches. Myrtle frowned. It almost seemed as if she *did* have an idea who could have done it, despite what she was saying.

"Maybe we can figure out who is responsible. Did you see or hear anything this morning when you were out walking dogs?" asked Myrtle, hoping that Rose would give her some sort of alibi.

Tears ran down Rose's pale cheeks and Buster the dog jumped up and put his paws on her to lick her face in concern. She put her arms around Buster and sobbed into his coat.

Myrtle jumped up. "Tissues! Tissues!" She hurried out of the living room to find a fresh box of tissues in the closet. She had the feeling that Rose might go through quite a few of them and that the half-empty box in the living room might not suffice.

She thrust the box at Rose who grabbed it. Rose handed Miles Buster's leash and then blindly stumbled back to the small hall that led to Myrtle's bathroom.

Myrtle and Miles stared at each other. Miles murmured, "She's a disaster."

"I haven't seen her for a while. She wasn't always this thin and pale." Myrtle glanced back to make sure Rose wasn't on her way back to the living room. "She's hiding something. I'm not sure that *she* did it, but I bet she knows who did," said Myrtle.

Rose returned, face red and eyes redder. She took Buster from Miles and sank down on the sofa, holding the leash limply.

She said, almost to herself, "I told Mother it was a bad idea. *Many* times."

"The book?" asked Miles.

Rose nodded absently. "She was bound and determined to put it out. Everyone has secrets, don't they? And things they feel guilty about?"

Myrtle and Miles obediently nodded, although Myrtle thought that her own secrets ran more along the lines of what gift she was purchasing for family for a birthday or Christmas. Or what activities she might be hiding from Red.

Rose continued, "No one wants their secrets exposed like that. Who wants secrets out in a book for everyone to see?"

Myrtle tried again. "Pearl seemed determined, I'll say that. But she didn't really tell us *why* she thought it was such a good idea to print your secrets. Only that it was healthier that way."

Rose said, "That's what she'd convinced herself of. She thought that the family would function so much better if everything was out in the open."

"It seems like a very extreme thing to do—steal a manuscript from a house in broad daylight. And then, of course, what happened to your mother," said Myrtle. "It seems . . . desperate."

Rose shook her head. "I can't imagine who could do such a thing. You're sure that the manuscript isn't somewhere here? That you didn't misplace it?"

This annoyed Myrtle, although she took pains not to show it. "I'm afraid I'm not as forgetful as all that," she said coolly.

Rose glanced across the room. "What about that pile of papers there?"

Miles winced. Myrtle did not like to be questioned like this. And she rarely lost things.

Myrtle gave Rose a tight smile. "Those are articles that I'm editing for the newspaper. An entirely different project. No, the unfortunate and inconvenient truth of the matter is that your mother brought me a book to edit. I left for lunch and left some windows open for my cat to come in and out. When I returned, the book was gone."

Rose nodded, looking miserable. "Sorry. I didn't mean to make it sound as though you'd lost it. I just hate the thought that someone I know would break into your home when you were doing a favor for Mother. I'd like to think that she simply tripped and fell down the stairs at home. She'd always go down the stairs too fast—I told her that over and over again. But if someone stole the book, that paints everything in a different light." She sighed and Buster looked at her with concern.

Finally, Rose said, "I should be going. Poor Buster hasn't had much of a walk."

Myrtle said, "Sweetie, how about if I give you your mother's meal that she brought by earlier today? She'd want you to have it."

Rose brightened. "Is it her chicken, broccoli, and rice?"

"It is indeed. And I insist. The last thing you want is to have to cook after a day like today," said Myrtle. "I have the perfect tote bag for you to carry it in."

"Thank you, Miss Myrtle," said Rose.

Rose and Miles ended up leaving simultaneously. "I'll talk with you later," said Miles as he left. Myrtle was already mentally writing her article for her editor, so just nodded in response.

After fifteen minutes, she'd nearly finished the first draft. There was a tap on her front door again and Myrtle rolled her eyes.

But when she opened the door, she saw Elaine and Jack there. Myrtle gave Elaine a smile before turning all her attention to Jack. "How's the best, smartest grandson ever?" asked Myrtle.

"Pasha here?" asked Jack, looking around for the cat.

"Not right this second, but I'm sure she could be here at any moment. She's been starving lately," said Myrtle. And, just to amuse the child, she opened a can of tuna in a very noisy fashion by the kitchen window. Sure enough, the black cat leapt through to Jack's delight.

"Remember to be gentle with Pasha," said Elaine in a warning tone.

"Smart advice. Although Pasha has a definite soft spot for Jack. They're both very, very bright, and Pasha recognizes that," said Myrtle, watching the two together.

Elaine hid a smile at Myrtle's recurring proclamation of the preschooler's brilliance. "I wanted to make sure you were okay, Myrtle. Red filled me in on what happened today and I know that you and Pearl were friends. Is everything all right?"

"Everything is most definitely *not* all right," said Myrtle. "Something was stolen from my house today and someone murdered my friend."

Elaine blinked at her. "Red somehow neglected to mention that," she said slowly.

"Red is apparently several steps behind me," said Myrtle brusquely. "I'm quickly coming to the conclusion that Jack's genius comes completely from you, Elaine."

"Can you fill me in?" asked Elaine.

Myrtle did, giving an animated version with lots of gestures to illustrate Pearl's visit, the theft of the manuscript, and the tragic discovery at Pearl's house.

Elaine frowned. "And Red isn't wanting to call it murder?"

"Well, naturally he'd prefer not to have the bother, right? No murder means no investigation, no state police, and more of a normal week. I know how busy Red is, and he'd rather skip all the extra work, I'm sure. Or, maybe he doesn't want to admit that I'm right about the fact that it was foul play and no tragic accident." Myrtle shrugged as if the workings of Red's thought processes were beyond her.

Elaine said, "I'm sure he'll come around soon, if he hasn't already." She glanced over at Myrtle's laptop, which was sitting on the table. "Are you working on a story for Sloan?" She squinted at the laptop and then winced. "I see the article covers Pearl's *murder*. Are you sure that Sloan will run that?"

Myrtle said in a lofty voice, "Sloan will run anything I say right now. He's so completely distracted and lovelorn that he isn't paying a bit of attention."

Elaine nodded. "I know what you mean. The poor guy. My freelance assignment over there is really taking off because he's not editing me at all. I just take pictures and stick them up on the *Bugle*'s social media sites."

Myrtle realized that it might be nice to have Elaine in her corner with the news story. "But do you know what this story needs? Pictures. That's the way to really bring it to life. You're ready to move from social media to print, Elaine. And this is the time and the story to do it."

Elaine's face lit up. "Do you think so, Myrtle?"

"I especially loved that picture you took of the largest tomato at the fair. The light was wonderful for that picture." Myrtle was glad she was able to come up with a sterling example of Elaine's abilities. Most of her pictures either had odd composition, weird shadows, were blurry, or displayed Elaine's omnipresent thumb. Apparently, it had been impossible to mess up the tomato picture.

Elaine beamed at her. "That *was* a good one, wasn't it? And Bernese was so pleased that her prize-winning tomato was on the *Bugle* Facebook account." Her face fell. "But Sloan hasn't given me the green light to take pictures for the paper itself. Only the social media accounts."

Myrtle said, "You haven't been paying attention, Elaine. Remember, Sloan is totally distracted with his romantic problems. You can do anything you like. If he *does* notice, you're welcome to blame it all on me"

Jack leaned over to give Pasha a kiss on the top of her head and the cat bumped her head against his in affectionate response.

Elaine seemed to accept this. "Okay," she said slowly. "But how do I take a picture that corresponds to your story on Pearl? It seems like I'd just be running an old picture of Pearl from the paper's archives or that I'd have to go over and take a picture of Pearl's house—and that wouldn't be very tactful at this point."

Myrtle frowned. She was right. It had to be something that wasn't too intrusive. If only she still had that manuscript. Then Elaine could take a picture of it as the element that spawned Pearl's murder. In Elaine's less-than-capable hands, the picture would be blurry anyway—perfect for being discreet.

Elaine brightened. "I know! I'll take a picture of you!"

Myrtle drew back a bit. "Of me?"

"Sure. After all, you're the reporter, the editor, and someone who was immediately at the scene when Pearl was discovered," said Elaine. She was already fumbling in her tote bag of a purse for her camera.

Myrtle was less pleased with this idea. She was never wild about being the subject of a photo, even in expert hands. She shuddered at the thought of what Elaine could make her look like. "Well, I don't know . . ."

"It's perfect! Here, sit at your table there, where your manuscript went missing. And look serious."

Myrtle plopped down at the table. The serious look came naturally as she watched Elaine pick up the camera and aim it in her general direction.

Elaine looked through the viewfinder. "Something's wrong with this thing," she muttered.

"The lens cap is still on," said Myrtle, somehow managing to repress a sigh.

"Silly of me," said Elaine with a laugh. "You can tell I didn't get much sleep last night."

Which would likely compound the problem. An inept photographer suffering from a lack of sleep.

"Perfect!" said Elaine as she took the picture. "Now, let me take a couple more." Jack came over to her and wrapped his arms around her leg as she balanced the camera and trained it on Myrtle.

"Your thumb is creeping over the lens," said Myrtle.

Elaine laughed again. "Oops. That finger is something of a scene-stealer."

She took the picture and then leaned back to inspect her work. "Oh, they came out great, Myrtle!"

Elaine showed them to Myrtle. Myrtle was pleased to see that they weren't as bad this time as she'd feared. Perhaps she was starting to catch on.

"And on the first try, too," said Myrtle. "Well then, that's all we need for the story, right? I'll go ahead and finish this up and then send it along to Sloan. Can you email the picture to him so that he'll have it to accompany my piece?"

Elaine nodded. "You'll email your article today, then?"

Myrtle said, "I'm not even sure that Sloan knows anything about Pearl's death. In this particular instance, I'm walking down there." She paused. "Just to let you know, I'll likely be purchasing a car. I'm getting tired of catching rides with others and sometimes walking doesn't agree with me."

Elaine just blinked at her. "Walking doesn't agree with you?"

"That's right. Oh, I don't mind it *sometimes*, but when you're carrying a cane, it's rather limiting in terms of what you can carry with your other hand. It used to be exercise. Now it's annoying." Myrtle made a face to indicate the level of annoyance that walking generated.

Elaine's face crumpled in worry. "Have you mentioned this to Red?"

"Of course not. Red's been too busy. Besides, it's none of Red's business what I spend my money on," said Myrtle a bit huffily.

Elaine slowly asked, "And, sorry for asking, but you do have the money for a car?"

Myrtle shook her head. "Not for a new car. But who wants a new car? No, I'm thinking of getting a used car. That way, it's already been broken in by someone else."

Elaine said, "This wouldn't have anything to do with Pearl's son owning a used car dealership, would it?"

"I was actually talking about it before then. Miles can corroborate. But it is an especially attractive prospect now, under the circumstances," said Myrtle.

"Just be careful," said Elaine. "Can't I just drive you down to see Sloan?"

Myrtle shook her head. "You have a million other things to do, Elaine. I'll be fine."

When Elaine left with Jack, Myrtle settled down to finish off her story and then edit it. In her own eyes, it was something of a masterpiece. She never came right out and said Pearl was murdered, but it was subtly implied.

She'd just finished revising the article and was printing it out for Sloan when her phone rang. Myrtle walked over to the wall phone in the kitchen and picked up. "Hello?"

A croaky voice grated, "Yer in danger."

Chapter Five

A smile pulled at Myrtle's lips. Wanda, an impoverished psychic who lived with her brother Crazy Dan, was a gifted seer and had become a friend. She was also Miles' cousin, much to his chagrin. "You're too late," said Myrtle crisply. "I've already had my home broken into and something important stolen."

Wanda said, "Still in danger now. Should walk away."

"You know better than that," said Myrtle.

Wanda sighed, a sound that devolved into a deep cough.

"You haven't started smoking again, have you?" asked Myrtle suspiciously.

"Naw. My lungs ain't so good, that's all," said Wanda. Then, "While yer at Sloan's, kin you give him my horoscopes?"

Wanda was writing the paper's horoscopes. They were wildly popular because of their specificity. She'd tell one resident to get his mower serviced and another to avoid driving a car on Tuesday. But Myrtle was the interpreter since Wanda was functionally illiterate. Myrtle bit back a sigh. This likely would take time.

Myrtle found a spiral notebook and poised her pen over the page, balancing the phone receiver on her shoulder. "Okay, shoot."

Wanda carefully detailed all the forthcoming events of the week. But when Miles was mentioned, Myrtle sighed. "Oh, Wanda. This will drive Miles nuts. He won't be any fun at all. In fact, if he reads this, he's likely to stay at home and not even answer his door."

Wanda's voice was determined. "He should know."

Myrtle looked at her notebook in dismay. Wanda had stated: *Miles. Germs is on their way. Beware.*

"You know that Miles is one step away from wearing a hazmat suit when he leaves home," said Myrtle fretfully. "He lays a handkerchief on chairs he thinks might be germy before he sits down. He carries hand sanitizer in his pockets at all times."

"Exactly why he's gonna get sick," said Wanda. "He ain't used to the germs like we is."

Myrtle groaned. "Okay, I guess the horoscope will have to run." It would run, but Myrtle had ideas for intercepting it before Miles saw it. She simply couldn't allow her sidekick to be sitting on the sidelines for this investigation. She was bound and determined to find out what happened to Pearl and who was responsible.

Wanda finished up her recitation of the horoscopes to come, thanked her, and signed off. Then Myrtle spent the next twenty minutes editing the horoscopes so they made sense. Finally, she set off for the *Bradley Bugle*.

When she arrived at the newspaper office, she pushed open the creaky wooden door to enter the paper-ridden newsroom. She glanced around. No Sloan. She waited for a few minutes, just in case Sloan perhaps had visited the restroom. No Sloan.

Myrtle frowned. She didn't have all day to hang around. Where could he be? He hadn't locked the door, so presumably he intended on returning. Then she thought of the little bar within walking distance of the newspaper office. She suspected that Sloan might well be there, drowning his sorrows. He wasn't ever averse to a drink and had certainly visited the bar in the past.

Myrtle walked over, the stories clutched in her hands. When she entered the bar, several of the patrons looked startled. A couple of her former students said, "Miss Myrtle!" as if she'd caught them misbehaving at school. She gave them a tight smile and they sat a little straighter in their chairs.

Sure enough, Sloan slumped on a barstool, morosely staring into a beer. The bar was playing mournful country songs which Myrtle was positive wasn't helping matters any.

"Sloan," she said crisply, carefully settling next to him at the bar. Fortunately, Myrtle was very tall and the barstool was the type with a back on it. She hung her cane from the bar.

Sloan jumped violently and then gaped at her. "Miss Myrtle!" he said, unconsciously parroting the other bar patrons. "What are you doing here?"

"I didn't see a sign saying *no octogenarian retired teachers allowed*," said Myrtle with a sniff. "Since I couldn't find you in the newsroom, I figured this might be a likely location."

Sloan was a mess. What was left of his hair was hanging in strands over his large and ever-expanding forehead. His eyes were bloodshot, whether from drinking or from crying, Myrtle wasn't sure. And she was fairly certain that Sloan wasn't on his first beer. However, he straightened up on his stool as she gave him the once-over.

Sloan seemed uncertain as to what to do. "Do you . . . well, do you want a drink, Miss Myrtle?"

"As a matter of fact, I do. It's been a horrid day." Myrtle turned to the bartender, whom she'd also taught, and glanced disapprovingly at the liquor bottles. "Do you have sherry here?"

The bartender scrambled around behind the bar. "Uh, just a second. I might." He pulled open cabinets both above and below the bar and triumphantly produced a dusty bottle.

"Might I have a very small glass?" asked Myrtle.

Sloan said, "You might as well have a very large one. I know you're not driving."

"Just because I had a bad day, there's no cause for getting sloppy," said Myrtle in a pointed tone. Sloan tucked his shirttail in, in response.

When Myrtle was served, she took a small sip and then said to Sloan, "Now what on earth is going on? Don't you have a paper to publish?"

Sloan groaned and put his head in his hands as if he had a toothache. "That's just the thing, Miss Myrtle. I don't know what happened to the day. At one point I looked at the clock and it was ten a.m. The next thing I knew, I looked at the clock and it was the end of the day."

"Whatever happened to the middle of the day? There's a whole lot more to the day than just ten and five," said Myrtle.

Sloan shrugged. "That's what I don't know. I tinkered with the paper . . . I definitely did that. Then I decided that maybe I should check what was going on with the paper's social media.

You know I have Elaine doing photos for us." He gave Myrtle a sideways glance.

"Don't worry, I'm completely aware that Elaine is a disaster as a photographer. Okay, so you went online to check the *Bugle's* Facebook and Twitter and whatnot. What happened then?" asked Myrtle.

"Well, then I got sort of distracted, I guess. I went over to look at Sally's social media because she posts on there a lot and I can get a good idea of her day. I saw what she'd eaten for breakfast and then when she left off for work," recited Sloan.

Myrtle broke in. "And that's when you fell asleep from sheer boredom?" she guessed.

He shook his head. "Wasn't boring to me. It just made me realize that if we were together, maybe I'd have been there with her during some of the stuff. Maybe we'd have eaten lunch together at the diner or somewhere. I guess the day just started flying by and I didn't even notice."

Myrtle said, "And tomorrow's edition of the newspaper?"

Sloan gave a small hiccup. "Once I realized it was too late to pull everything together, I decided to jump ship and come here."

Myrtle said sternly, "It is *not* too late. You have all the material and just need to put it together."

Sloan looked sorrowfully at Myrtle. "I don't think I can. Was just going to tell everybody that the press went down and that's why we didn't run."

Myrtle glowered at him. "It is *not* too late. How many times do I have to say it? My word, you sound just like you did back in school when you didn't hand your homework in. Don't you know it's better to be late than not publish it at all?"

"Folks won't miss one little paper," said Sloan.

Myrtle decided that it was a sign of his current intoxication that he argued with her at all. Usually she made him shake in his shoes.

Myrtle leaned forward. "Let's recap this. You spent the entire day getting sucked into social media online. Then you realized that the paper wasn't done. Then you came to a *bar*?"

Sloan considered this. "That's about the long and the short of it, yes."

"Well, the people of the good town of Bradley are expecting their newspaper tomorrow. The newspaper that *they paid for*. What will they do for direction in their lives without Wanda's words of advice?" demanded Myrtle.

Sloan said, "I don't know if Wanda's horoscopes technically qualify as advice."

"When she tells someone not to water their grass seed because it's going to rain? That's not advice?" Myrtle's voice crept higher and the former pupils in the bar shifted nervously in response.

"Okay, I guess you're right. But they can skip it for one day," mumbled Sloan.

Myrtle took a large sip of her small sherry. "What about the fact that there's a huge news story that people are going to be looking for?"

Sloan frowned. "What story is that? Did Mildred actually win the peach cobbler prize at the fair finally?"

Myrtle said, "It's a testament to your total absorption in losing Sally that you're even asking this. Apparently, you haven't heard the news that Pearl Epps is dead?"

Sloan blinked at her. "No. Oh, gosh. You're right—that *is* a story. Everybody knows Pearl."

"Not only that, but Pearl was murdered—likely by someone in her own family," said Myrtle. She took another sip of the sherry.

"Murdered!" Sloan gaped at her again.

"That's right, murdered. Except I had to be fairly subtle in the writing of the story since that fact isn't yet accepted from all corners," said Myrtle.

"You have a story ready to run?" asked Sloan, sounding more interested and engaged now.

"I certainly do. Not only that, but Elaine has taken a photo to accompany the article and has emailed it to you," said Myrtle.

Sloan looked gloomy and Myrtle hastened to add, "It's actually a good picture."

Sloan glanced at his watch and sighed. "Guess I better get with it, then."

"I'll help you compile the paper for an hour or so. But let's get on with it," said Myrtle briskly.

She rummaged in her purse for her money, but Sloan stopped her. "No, ma'am. I've got this. It's the least I can do. The paper should be reliable. You're absolutely right."

An hour later and after Myrtle felt fairly assured that the newspaper would indeed be coming out the following day, Myrtle set off for home, thumping her cane on the ground emphatically as she went. About a hundred yards from the newspaper office, she felt a familiar furriness brush against her leg and looked down to see Pasha walking closely next to her.

Myrtle beamed at the black cat. "You kept an eye out for me, didn't you, Pasha? What a brilliant little animal you are."

A voice from behind her drawled, "Nonsense. With all the thumping you do with that cane that cat could hear you from a mile away."

Myrtle turned to glare at Red who was slowly driving alongside her in his police cruiser. "Don't you have anything better to do than to harass your poor mother? Like investigate a murder?"

Red said mildly, "Now Mama, I'll admit that the state police have reached the conclusion that Pearl's was a suspicious death. I'd like to have a quick word with you about Pearl's visit and what happened when you and Miles returned from lunch."

Myrtle pressed her lips together in annoyance as she continued making her way home. Finally, she said, "I suppose that's fine. You'll have to wait for me to walk back, though. I can't relay a story like this from the sidewalk."

"I can give you a lift if you'd just stop for a second," said Red, irritation in his voice.

"That might be fine for me, but I doubt Pasha would care for it," said Myrtle.

"Pasha is outside seventy-five percent of the time. I'm pretty sure she can find her way to your house if you catch a ride with me." Red's voice was getting that tight sound.

Myrtle said, "But she's hungry. I can tell when the cat wants something to eat. Pasha won't be happy losing sight of me when she wants cat food. Of course, when I have my own car, I can slowly get Pasha accustomed to being inside a carrier in the car. She'll make a good passenger with some training."

There was a brief, stunned silence before Red growled, "Car?"

"Didn't I tell you?" asked Myrtle, turning to look innocently at him. "I decided that I'm having to do far too much walking and far too much asking for rides from very busy people. You and Elaine are always in the middle of something important or taking Jack somewhere. It would be better if I had my own car and could simply drive whenever I wanted to."

"Mama, you haven't driven in years!"

"You know that isn't true. I regularly borrow Miles's car when he's unable to drive me himself," said Myrtle stiffly.

"Regularly? More like once every few months," said Red.

"Which still qualifies as regularly," said Myrtle.

Red looked as though he very much wanted to pursue this conversation, but also wanted to get some information from Myrtle on what had transpired earlier in the day.

"I'll meet you at the house," he muttered and drove on ahead of her.

When Myrtle got home, she let both Red and Pasha in and then busied herself making Pasha some food.

"The cat's not expecting, is she?" asked Red suspiciously as Pasha gulped down the food in more of a canine than feline fashion.

"I had her fixed, if you'll recall. Elaine helped me trap her," said Myrtle shortly. She was still annoyed about the car. Although she had no *real* plans to purchase one, she wanted to assert her independence. It was most annoying when Red pushed back.

"Why is she inhaling her food then?" Red watched as Pasha finished her food and sat back, licking her paw and then scrubbing her face with it.

"Because she's eliminated her natural food source," said Myrtle, still sounding cranky.

Red frowned at her.

"Nature," Myrtle elaborated, pointing toward the window. "Birds, snakes, bats, mice, shrews. Pasha is too good at hunting."

Red tilted his head to one side in thought. "Come to think of it, I haven't been awakened by the birds too often lately."

Myrtle shrugged. "Pasha has seriously eliminated the population."

"Shouldn't you keep her in the house, then? It sounds like she's creating some sort of environmental imbalance." Red watched as Pasha now started giving herself a general bath, purring all the time.

"Except that she's feral. Pasha doesn't belong to me. I'm helping by giving her more to eat. Maybe she'll feel less-motivated to go hunt if it's only for sport. Now, you wanted to talk to me about the murder?" asked Myrtle, pointedly glancing at her watch.

Red sighed. "I'm willing to concede that it was a murder. I had a little voice inside me that thought it was murder this morning."

"That little voice needs a megaphone," said Myrtle crisply.

Red continued as if she hadn't spoken. "The thing is, if anybody had asked me who the least-likely person in Bradley was to get murdered, I'd have said Pearl Epps."

"Not me?" asked Myrtle in fake hurt.

Red snorted. "You'd win the prize of *most* likely to be murdered, Mama. You have people coming after you all the time when you're snooping around."

Myrtle said, "Well, apparently Pearl is *not* the least-likely person to be murdered. Maybe she was before she wrote her memoir."

Red plopped down on her sofa and opened up his little notebook. "Right. Now, about this book of hers. Did you happen to read any of the pages?"

Myrtle shook her head. "Not really. I glanced through part of it, but mostly just to scan for punctuation and obvious grammatical issues. I wanted to see how much work it would be to edit a book for her."

"You didn't get a feel as to why somebody would be desperate to get hold of those papers?" asked Red.

"No. Did you have any luck finding Pearl's computer?"

"Nope." Red sighed. "I have the feeling that it's at the bottom of the lake now."

"So it *was* missing," said Myrtle in a smug tone.

Red sighed again. "That's right. We searched the house, and it definitely wasn't there. Hubert agreed that it was missing. I sure wish I knew what was in that book."

"Secrets," said Myrtle with a shrug.

"But what *kind* of secrets?"

"Does it even matter?" asked Myrtle. "Something that Pearl's family didn't want aired in public."

Red said, "I just can't imagine what kind of secrets Pearl's family could have. That Hubert prefers Froot Loops for breakfast? That Rose is allergic to dogs, even though she's a dog walker?"

Myrtle said, "One would assume it's simply dirty laundry that Pearl's family didn't want aired in a small town."

"Okay. Moving on to the theft of this book. How did someone get into your house?" Red's eyes narrowed as he glanced around the room.

"It's hardly Fort Knox here, Red. But as I mentioned earlier, most likely they came in through the windows. I had them open for Pasha."

Red glared at the windows as if they'd personally affronted him. He growled, "I take this very personally. Some joker broke into the police chief's elderly mother's house. A police chief who, I might add, lives right across the street. In broad daylight. It's insulting."

"You're making me sound feeble, Red," said Myrtle.

"I said *elderly*. Not feeble."

Myrtle said flatly, "The break-in was no big deal. It was simply something of a surprise."

"You'd have been a lot *more* surprised if you'd walked in on a robbery in progress," said Red.

Myrtle put her nose in the air. "I'd have been perfectly fine. I can take care of myself as I've proven before. Besides, I had Miles with me."

Red rolled his eyes. "You're right, Mama. I don't know what I was thinking."

He closed his notebook and then tapped his pen against it thoughtfully. "It seems to me that I remember something about the Epps family from a long time ago. Am I imaging that?"

"You're imagining it," said Myrtle. She paused. "Oh, wait. I know what you're talking about, but it didn't directly involve the family. It was decades ago . . . actually, when you were a teenager."

Red snapped his fingers. "That's right. It was a big deal at the time, though. A girl ran away from home, didn't she? Tonya? Tina?"

Chapter Six

"Tara," said Myrtle. Her expression became thoughtful. "I taught her, as a matter of fact."

"Naturally," said Red. "Can you remember what happened to her? She ran away from home, didn't she?"

"And hasn't been seen or heard from since. There was some investigation at the time and that's probably why you remember the Epps family being involved. Tara was Rose's best friend," said Myrtle.

"I'll look in the old files. That's odd they wouldn't have put more time into the disappearance of a young person," said Red, frowning.

Myrtle said slowly, "The theory at the time was that Tara had been somewhat troubled and had threatened to run away before. But her parents never got over it. They moved away years ago."

Red strode toward the door.

"What are you doing now?" asked Myrtle.

Red said, "I'm going to ask the one person who spies on everybody in the neighborhood if she saw anybody hanging out of the windows at your house."

Myrtle made a face. "Erma Sherman! Ugh. That's a waste of your time."

Red said, "How do you figure that? We're talking about the woman who is so nosy about everybody's business that she asked me the other day if Jack was feeling any better. She'd seen me come home and then leave again and bring in a bag from the pharmacy." He shook his head.

"But if Erma knew something about a break-in at my house, do you think that she'd be content to sit silently at home? No. She'd be hootin' and hollerin' at the person until somebody came over and hauled the burglar out."

Red considered this.

Myrtle continued, "And then she'd have told everybody in town later how she saved the day and how she looks out for her poor, decrepit neighbor, Myrtle. She'd pressure the town of Bradley to give her a medal and throw a tickertape parade."

Red hid a smile that threatened to tug at his lips. "That's true."

"Believe me, she doesn't know a thing," said Myrtle emphatically.

Red said, "That may be the case, but I still need to drop by and talk to her. Maybe she saw someone lingering on the street. Maybe she noticed a car that isn't usually here."

"Or maybe she has one of her frequent and disgusting illnesses and spent the entire morning in her bathroom," growled Myrtle. "It's my understanding that she's been sick."

"Still, I need to go by there. You be careful, Mama, and leave those windows shut for now. Let Pasha scratch on the door if she needs something." He hesitated and then gave her a light kiss on the cheek. This completely stunned Myrtle to silence.

"See you later, Mama," said Red as he left.

Myrtle sat for a few minutes and then got up to pick up the phone. "Sloan? It's Myrtle. It's definitely murder now, so just take out my subtlety and any ambiguity. Somebody shoved poor Pearl down those stairs."

That night, Myrtle slept fitfully. She got out of bed at 3:30 and made herself a large breakfast. It was, she decided, a testament to her general sangfroid that when a figure appeared in her kitchen window while she was scrambling eggs, she didn't immediately jump to the conclusion that it was a burglar. Instead, she calmly opened the window and let Pasha in.

"What a bright girl!" crooned Myrtle as she opened a can of cat food. She frowned. The stock of cat food in her pantry was running lower than she'd thought. But today was the day of the sale. She just needed to make sure that someone could drive her to the grocery store. There was no way for her to handle a walk home with a cane and a large amount of canned cat food. She had the feeling that Red would be too busy to accommodate her. Elaine might be too if she was out doing photo assignments for the newspaper. Even Miles might be an issue if she didn't intercept his morning newspaper with that horoscope in it.

After eating a very large breakfast of eggs, sausage, and a bowl of grits, Myrtle heard a car and looked outside. Sure enough, it was the paper being delivered. She hurried outside to see what Sloan had managed to put in today's edition.

He'd done a fairly decent job turning Myrtle's story into more of a crime story and less of a retrospective on Pearl's life.

Fortunately, she didn't see any sign of typos in the copy. Then she glanced through the rest of the paper. There were the horoscopes and Miles's warning from Wanda to beware of germs. She sighed. She'd simply walk over there really quickly and intercept the newspaper before he even realized it was out there. Then she'd suggest later that she give him her paper to read so he wouldn't call Sloan about the delivery problem. Myrtle supposed that she'd need to have a terrible accident involving a large cup of coffee and the horoscope section.

She slipped on a long robe and slid into a pair of hard-soled slippers. Then she proceeded into the night with Pasha following closely at her side. She stumbled a little over a crumbly part of the sidewalk and let out an annoyed cry. Someone in public works needed to do something about the state of the sidewalks.

She had picked up Miles's newspaper when there was a shout from behind her. "Stop! Thief!"

Myrtle, clutching at the newspaper, frowned and glanced at the surrounding houses to see if she saw any burglars.

Then a figure ran in front of her and came to a complete stop.

The figure had just raised her arms in front of her to stop Myrtle's progress when it dropped them. "Myrtle!" said the figure, her despised neighbor, Erma.

Myrtle sighed. "What's this all about, Erma?"

A light in Miles's front room turned on and his front door opened. "Who's out there?" he asked suspiciously.

Erma bellowed, "It's just Myrtle. She took your newspaper. I thought it was that burglar that Red was telling me about yesterday. Just trying to keep our elderly residents safe, that's all. I've barely slept a wink for worrying about it. Which is a shame since I have this awful health condition right now."

A voice from one of the neighboring houses called out, "Can you take it inside? No one can get any sleep!"

"The nerve of some people," said Erma in a huffy voice.

"I *wasn't* taking your newspaper, Miles. I was only collecting it on my way in for a visit." Myrtle glared at Erma.

Miles, who had shifted his weight from side to side when the neighbor complained, quickly said, "Let's just come inside."

Erma's eyebrows shot up in surprise. "Me, too?"

Myrtle said, "Not you! I have something I want to discuss in private with Miles."

Erma said in a knowing voice, "Ohhhh, I see. Well, don't let me disturb the two lovebirds." Then she paused. "How about if I just come in for a few minutes before you discuss your private business? I'd like to ask what happened with Pearl yesterday."

Which was when Pasha, who'd leapt out of sight when Erma came charging up, returned, hissing and growling at her. Erma, allergic to cats, turned and hurried toward her house. "See ya later," she blurted.

Miles opened the door wider to let Myrtle in and gazed anxiously into the darkness outside. "Is Pasha coming in?"

Myrtle led the way into Miles's kitchen. "I doubt it. She's already had her walk and then did her good deed for the day by scaring Erma off. The poor cat probably needs a nap now."

Myrtle carefully put the newspaper in front of her on the counter as she made the coffee.

"Do you want anything to eat?" asked Miles. "I do have some of those good biscuits from the Piggly Wiggly."

"Let's have biscuits and coffee then." Myrtle was more concerned about keeping Miles occupied than in eating. She needed him to be thinking about plates, warming the biscuits, and getting out butter and knives until she was able to make sure that his horoscope was out of commission. And despite the fact that she'd just eaten a large breakfast, she figured she could still manage to eat a biscuit.

But apparently Erma and the odd encounter outside was still on his mind.

"So you were just bringing in my paper for me?" asked Miles as he got the plates out.

"The newspaper? Yes. I couldn't sleep and decided to come over. I figured picking up your paper was the least I could do in exchange for coffee and breakfast," said Myrtle graciously.

Miles said, "I wasn't sleeping well, either. So the newspaper—was your story in there?"

"The story is in there. Oh, and I had a visit from Red last night."

"Did he tell you not to get a car?" asked Miles, trying unsuccessfully to hide a smile.

Myrtle said, "He might have mentioned something about not getting one, although, that has very little importance since he has no control whether I get a car or not."

Miles said, "I suspect that you really don't *want* a car. You haven't really wanted one before. You're just bored and stirring up trouble."

Myrtle took out the coffee mugs. "I can't imagine what may have given you that idea, Miles. I'm planning on going to the used car dealership later today, as a matter of fact."

Miles said, "The one owned by Boone Epps?" He gave Myrtle a knowing look. "I'm assuming not the other used car lot here."

Myrtle shrugged. "It seems like serendipity, doesn't it? I mention being interested in a used car. The next thing I know, a friend of mine is murdered, and her son happens to own a used car dealership."

Miles was busying himself with putting the butter on the table. Myrtle took the opportunity to destroy Miles's newspaper with coffee by knocking the paper into the sink and then pouring coffee all over it.

"Mercy!" cried out Myrtle.

Miles turned as Myrtle held up the sopping wet paper over the sink.

Myrtle said, "Sorry. I don't know what happened. One minute I was pouring coffee into a mug and the next the newspaper was knocked in the way."

Miles picked up his trashcan and moved it to the sink. "No point in trying to read that, Myrtle. Just throw it away. I'll look at yours later."

Myrtle said, "And of course I'd *want* you to look at mine later. It's such a pity that the paper delivery guy skipped me today."

Miles nodded slowly, looking at Myrtle through narrowed eyes. "Okay. Well, let's have our biscuits. Do you need to make more coffee?"

"Oh, no. No, there's enough for us to both have a cup." Because Myrtle had made more than she'd needed to for this very reason.

They settled down at Miles's kitchen table and spent a few moments in companionable silence. Then Miles said, "So if Red *wasn't* there to warn you off buying a car, what was he there for?"

Myrtle finished a bite of her biscuit. "He admitted that Pearl was murdered. There were apparently signs of a struggle."

"Poor Pearl," said Miles.

"I just get madder and madder over the whole thing," said Myrtle.

Miles asked, "Did the police find her computer?"

"No. Someone took a lot of trouble to make sure that her memoir is gone. The laptop is likely at the bottom of the lake somewhere," said Myrtle.

Miles said, "Pearl's life was clearly more faceted than anyone gave her credit for."

They drank their coffee and enjoyed the quiet until Miles said in a cheerful tone, "At least we saw Rose yesterday. That means there's no need to cook a casserole and tote it over."

Myrtle said, "There is likely still a need for a casserole."

"I'm quite certain there's not," said Miles.

"Not for Rose, I mean. But there are others in that family who we might need an excuse for a conversation with," said Myrtle.

Miles frowned. "I'm not as well-acquainted with the family tree. I thought it was simply a matter of Pearl and Hubert and their children, Rose and Boone."

"There is also Pearl's sister, Nell," said Myrtle.

Miles said, "Nell Prentiss?"

"You know her?" Myrtle finished off her biscuit.

Miles tempered this. "I don't really know Nell. She is part of that Scrabble club that I've had to play with from time to time."

"Ah. The one Maisy dragged you into," said Myrtle with a smile.

Miles said stiffly, "I'm hardly playing at all. I'm just on the alternates list for when a regular can't make it."

"If you were *me*, you wouldn't be on it at all," said Myrtle. "I know how to say no."

Miles said, "If I recall, you weren't *asked* to be in the Scrabble club."

"That's because I win every time," said Myrtle. "It eliminates the fun factor."

"Anyway," said Miles, trying to return to the original point, "Nell is part of that club. What do you know of her?"

Myrtle said, "She's Pearl's older sister and never married. Is she one of the ladies who's trying to catch you?"

Miles gave Myrtle a cold look. "Catch me?"

"Yes. You know, that band of merry widows who drop by with food and laugh too loudly when you're around. Not that Nell is a widow, just that she might be part of that flirty group."

Miles said, "She is not part of that flirty group. Be aware that I'm not necessarily agreeing, by the way, that such a group exists."

"We should see Nell this morning," said Myrtle. "She might know what was going on in Pearl's family."

"It sounds like she's *in* Pearl's family. Maybe she's a suspect, too," said Miles.

Myrtle looked doubtful. "Secrets about Nell? I can't imagine what those could be."

Miles said, "Hasn't everyone said the same about Pearl? And her life was apparently rife with secrets."

"I suppose."

Miles said, "Why don't you just speak to Nell in a reporter guise?"

Myrtle snorted. "Nell would slam the door on me. She has quite the no-nonsense manner. No, it needs to be food and sympathy."

Miles's face creased in worry before he suddenly brightened and snapped his fingers. "I know! There's a great new ready-to-eat meal in the Piggly Wiggly deli. I tried it just the other day. It was beef stroganoff with a side of wild rice. Very tasty. You could put it on your own plate."

Myrtle sniffed. "Good try, Miles, but I hardly think Nell Prentiss will have the same culinary leanings as a bachelor. I'll prepare my famous cassoulet."

"Dare I ask why it's famous?" asked Miles gloomily.

"Don't be rude. It's delicious," said Myrtle firmly. She frowned. "If I can locate the cookbook. I haven't made my famous cassoulet for a while."

Miles raised his eyebrows. "I find it hard to believe that you lose track of anything in your house. It's very tidy and organized in there."

"Yes, but Red came over one day last year and insisted that a friend of his wanted to borrow some old cookbooks. He carefully picked out about half a dozen and then left with them. He never returned them." Myrtle frowned at the memory.

Miles said, "And the name of the friend who wanted the old cookbooks?"

"Undisclosed," replied Myrtle curtly.

Miles made some odd expressions while keeping his mouth from turning up at the corners.

"It doesn't matter. I can make the recipe by heart," said Myrtle.

Miles said, "That doesn't sound like a very good idea. Why don't you just focus on your chicken and broccoli? That's pretty basic."

"You're missing the point, Miles. This is supposed to be a work of art—a physical manifestation of my sympathy for Nell."

"I thought it was supposed to be a way for us to have a conversation with her without having a door slammed in our faces," said Miles.

Myrtle was too absorbed in her thoughts to hear him. "I should get started."

"But it's five in the morning. What time does Nell get up in the morning?"

Myrtle shrugged. "I suppose she should be ready for a visit by ten a.m. Does anyone ever really sleep the night after their sister is murdered?"

Myrtle grabbed her cane and strode back to Miles's front door.

"Thanks for the visit," said Miles dryly.

Myrtle nodded absently in return.

Chapter Seven

B ut at ten o'clock, when Myrtle and Miles were ringing Nell's doorbell, she drove into her driveway. Nell's house was conveniently located on Magnolia Lane, the same as Myrtle's and Miles's.

"See? Nell has already been out today. Other people in town are early birds," said Myrtle with a sniff. She carefully juggled the cassoulet and gave Nell a jaunty wave.

"Not to be rude, Myrtle, but that casserole smells odd," said Miles.

"It's simply your unrefined senses," said Myrtle in a firm voice. "And it's not a casserole. It's a *cassoulet.*"

"How did you get hold of duck this early in the morning?" asked Miles. His eyes narrowed suspiciously.

"Duck? Oh, one bird is as good as another," said Myrtle airily as Nell parked her car in the garage.

Miles said, "Does that mean that you used chicken?"

"Why not?" asked Myrtle.

"As I recall, that recipe has *lots* of ingredients in it. Like pork shoulder," said Miles.

"A mere technicality," said Myrtle.

"You substituted . . . what? Hot dogs?" asked Miles. He shuddered.

"Certainly not! Have you lost your mind?" hissed Myrtle. "I used pork barbeque. I happened to have some in my fridge from the other day."

Miles took a deep breath and then released it. "You really whipped this meal up in a flash. Doesn't cassoulet usually take days to prepare?"

"Only for beginners," said Myrtle tersely.

Nell got out of her car, looking curiously at them and the covered dish in Myrtle's hands. "Myrtle? Miles? Can I help you?" she asked briskly.

Myrtle said quickly, "It's more of us running by to see if *we* can help *you*. We're so sorry about poor Pearl."

Nell pressed her lips together and then said, "Thanks. I'm still trying to absorb it all. Please, won't you come in?"

It was the kind of perfunctory statement that you make when you hope that the other person will quickly just hand you the covered dish and be on their way.

Myrtle quickly said, "That would be wonderful, Nell, thank you."

Nell gave a resigned nod as she led them inside. "Sorry about the state of the house. There will still be a cereal dish out and about somewhere. I had to leave early to be at the church." She took the dish from Myrtle and quickly took it into the kitchen. "Are you feeling better, Myrtle? I heard you were doing poorly."

Myrtle gritted her teeth and then said, "I'm just fine, thanks. It's apparently just a rumor that someone started."

When Nell returned, Miles said, "We're sorry we're here so early. Were you planning Pearl's service?"

Nell gestured for them to sit down, which they did on well-worn antiques. "No. That is, Pearl's service is being planned, but that's not why I was at the church today. I'm one of the bell-ringers and we had a practice."

Myrtle said, "I didn't realize that you did that, Nell. I'm sure the church really appreciates your help. Even when I'm not at church, I always enjoy hearing the bells."

Nell looked pleased. "It's fun for me. Actually, that's the only way that I'm really involved at the church. I just love ringing and I love the other bell-ringers. We're like a little family."

Myrtle nodded and then said, "Speaking of family, I just wanted to let you know how very sorry I was for what happened with Pearl."

Nell's face drew into tight lines. "Thank you." She paused for a moment, looking blankly around the room with its faded wallpaper and worn furniture. Then she said to Myrtle, "I understand that Pearl reached out to you yesterday."

Myrtle said, "She did. And I agreed to give her a hand. As a matter of fact, Miles was there, too."

Nell sighed. "I feel terrible that *I* wasn't around yesterday morning. I hate the thought that my sister needed help, and I wasn't there to give it. I knew this morning would be an early day for the bell-ringing practice, so I'd slept in yesterday. Then I slowly got ready for the day and had a late breakfast and a late crossword."

Nell gestured at the crossword. "As you can see, it's a habit of mine. Although, unfortunately, not much of an alibi for your son," she said, looking at Myrtle.

Myrtle made a face. "You know that Red and I don't always see things eye-to-eye, Nell. You didn't know that you needed an alibi, did you?"

Miles said, "Looks as if you ran out of time to finish your crossword today."

Nell snorted. "More like I ran out of knowledge to finish it." She saw him looking at it and said, "Go ahead and take a stab at it. I could use the help. For some reason, I seem to be better at Scrabble than I am at crosswords, at least lately."

Miles didn't need to be told twice. He picked up the newspaper and the pen beside it as Myrtle gritted her teeth. She hoped that Miles would stick with the crossword and not venture over to the horoscopes.

"Did you know much about Pearl's memoir?" asked Myrtle.

Nell glanced away. "Not really. None of us thought Pearl would be able to *finish* a book. You know how it is—people always say that they want to write a book or that they've started a book. But how many folks have the discipline to go all the way through to the end?"

Myrtle glanced over at Miles. He was tapping the pen against his leg and frowning at the crossword puzzle.

Nell followed her glance and said to Miles, "It's hard today, isn't it? It's not just me?"

"It's as if some sort of crossword PhD took over the puzzle today," said Miles seriously.

Myrtle was determined to get the conversation away from puzzles and newspapers altogether. She glared at Miles as if to remind him of the purpose of their visit. But Miles was already idly thumbing through the paper, taking special interest in Myrtle's story.

Nell said, "You wrote a good article today, Myrtle. It was a nice tribute to Pearl, too." Nell started to tear up, but then rapidly blinked her eyes to force any of the intrepid tears from pouring out. Myrtle had no need to worry about Nell losing it. She was a trooper.

Myrtle said, "Thanks. I hoped it was. Pearl was a good friend and I can't believe that she's gone. Going back to her book—clearly, the family was surprised that she actually set her mind to it and finished it."

"That's right," said Nell. "But I don't know why we were surprised. This was *Pearl*. She could do anything. She could run five committees at church, create a magazine-worthy English garden at her home, and knit blankets for children's hospitals on the side. If anyone would be able to finish a book, it would be Pearl."

Myrtle said, "Did Pearl talk at all about what she'd written?"

Nell pressed her lips shut tightly again as if to keep unwanted words from flying out. She said, "Not really. I suppose everyone has things about themselves or their family that no one really knows about. Maybe that sort of thing would be interesting to others."

Myrtle gave Miles a nervous glance. He was now on the page with the horoscopes and completely absorbed. Then he froze and leveled a cold stare at Myrtle.

Myrtle frowned at her. "That's hardly the sort of thing that would make someone break into my house to steal a manuscript."

"You're taking it rather personally, aren't you?" asked Nell in frigid tones.

"Having my house broken into *is* personal," said Myrtle. Her eyes were steely.

Miles was now removing antibacterial wipes from his pocket and very carefully wiping his hands in a surreptitious manner. Myrtle sighed.

Nell rubbed at her shoulder absently as if it hurt. "The truth is that I don't know what the truth is. I'm simply concerned about my family and don't want to see more harm come to them. Rose, as I'm sure you could tell, is very delicate. Very fragile."

Myrtle said, "I thought she appeared to be under a lot of stress and had had a terrible shock with the death of her mother. She certainly was functioning, though. She was walking a client's dog when we spoke with her."

Nell nodded. "That's all true. But the fact of the matter is that she's been that way for a while now. Whatever stress she's under is messing with her brain. She can't remember *anything* and she's in middle age. *I* have a better memory than she does and I don't have a good one at all. But I don't know of any reason why Rose would be concerned about her mother publishing a memoir. And I don't know of any reason why Boone or Hubert would be concerned, either." But Nell looked away again as she said it.

Miles was now sitting with his hands carefully folded in his lap as if to avoid any further contact with bacteria in Nell's tidy home.

"Did Pearl and Boone get along well?" asked Myrtle.

Nell gave her a sharp look. "Mothers and sons usually get along quite well, don't they? It's said that they share a special relationship."

Myrtle said, "Sometimes they do and sometimes they don't."

Miles smiled.

Nell was quiet for a moment and then said, "I wouldn't have said that Boone and Pearl got along *perfectly*, but they were very fond of each other. Pearl always seemed very proud of Boone and the success he's made of his life."

Myrtle said, "My own son's fondest wish is to lock me away in Greener Pastures Retirement Home. I can assure you that *we* don't get along perfectly, either. In fact, we have prodigious arguments nearly weekly."

Nell said, "I'd just say that Boone and Pearl seemed at odds with each other lately. Pearl had had a few minor mishaps in her car and Boone thought that she needed to stop driving. Maybe let Hubert drive her around to errands and so forth. But Pearl was very independent and wanted to keep driving. She didn't want to ask Hubert to drop her off at choir practice or to run by the library. Pearl wanted to set her own timetable for her day and not have to plan it around when Hubert could drive her. Boone wanted her safe and Pearl wanted her freedom. It was all completely understandable." Nell held out her hands as if to display the utter reasonableness of their arguments.

Myrtle said, "And none of these disagreements revolved around Pearl's book?"

"Not that I was aware. Of course, I wasn't always around," said Nell.

Miles, sensing a lull in the conversation, stood up. "We should probably go and let Nell get on with her day."

Myrtle raised her eyebrows. "All right. Nell, it was good to see you, but sorry it was under these circumstances."

Nell nodded and said to Miles, "Maybe we'll see each other at Scrabble soon."

Miles gave her a tight smile. Myrtle imagined that he was imagining what a chore it would be to use antibacterial wipes on all of those tiny tiles.

Once Myrtle and Miles were outside, Miles hissed at her, "What was the big idea, trying to keep me away from my horoscope?"

"What, that silly thing?" Myrtle made a dismissive gesture with her hand. "You don't mean you put any stock into those things."

"Only when Wanda writes them," said Miles. "Which she did. And Wanda called me out specifically and referenced germs." He shuddered.

"And there are likely many places where you should heed her advice. Perhaps if we visit someone at the hospital. Or if we go to Wanda's house. But any germ with half a brain wouldn't be in Nell Prentiss's house. That place was scrubbed within an inch of its life. And she apologized for the mess." Myrtle snorted.

Miles said gloomily, "Well, I suppose we'll find out soon enough if I've contracted something horrible."

"If you believe you're going to contract something horrible, it's Erma Sherman you should be avoiding. She's constantly attempting to fill me in on whatever horrendous condition she has." Myrtle jumped as her phone rang. "That ringer is set way too high."

"Hello?" she asked briskly as she and Miles headed down the street toward her house.

A wretched coughing emanated from the phone, causing Miles to shrink away from Myrtle as if he could be somehow contaminated.

Myrtle frowned. "Wanda? Is that you?"

Wanda croaked out, "Me." Then she set about to coughing again.

"You sound terrible," scolded Myrtle. "You need to see a doctor."

Wanda's response to this was to engage in another fit of coughing.

"We'll pick you up and take you to the doctor," said Myrtle. "They will need to check that out." She paused and then asked cautiously, "Do you have insurance of some sort?"

Wanda finished coughing and then croaked again, "I got somethin' they'll take."

"I suppose that will have to do, whatever that is. Which doctor do you see?" asked Myrtle.

"Don't regularly see one," said Wanda in an offhanded way.

"All right. Not the right way to go about it, though. When you *do*, sporadically, happen to see someone, who do you see?" Myrtle fumbled for her keys as she and Miles reached her doorstep.

Some more coughing. Then Wanda said, "Ain't seen nobody since I was a kid."

"For heaven's sake! All right. Let me call up my own physician and explain the circumstances. Maybe he can fit you in. I taught the man and it's the least he can do for the trouble he caused me in the classroom. Miles and I will pick you up."

Miles looked panicked at this and shook his head violently. "Germs."

Myrtle sighed. "Never mind. *I* will drive over and pick you up in Miles's car and we'll go to the doctor."

Wanda gave a chuckle that rapidly turned into a hacking cough. Finally, she said, "Germs."

"That's right. And I'll have to give you a piece of my mind about that horoscope when you're feeling better. I'll call you back as soon as I've talked to the doctor's office," said Myrtle.

She hung up and pushed open her door. "Coming in?" she asked as Miles hesitated in the doorway. "Oh, come on, you don't think that *my house* is contaminated, do you? Wanda should have had the foresight to give a much more detailed prediction, especially considering the recipient."

"Wanda *never* gives detailed predictions," said Miles wearily as he entered the house and pulled out a bottle of hand sanitizer from his pants pocket.

Myrtle said, "Let's face it, Miles. If my house were to confer germs on you, it would have already happened. You've spent a good deal of time here and haven't yet fallen ill." She plopped down in her armchair and pulled out her phone, frowning at her contact list. "Here we are."

Miles cautiously sat in the next armchair as if the piece of furniture might bite him. "You know Dr. Frazier isn't taking any new patients."

"Well, that's a completely ridiculous mindset for a small town. Where are the sick people supposed to go, then? There's only one other doctor and he's *also* limiting new patients. If it keeps going on like this, the sick people won't have anyone to see and they'll just circulate among us, infecting others. Like zombies," said Myrtle in a distracted voice as she punched the keyboard to dial the doctor.

This was perhaps not the ideal image to draw up in Miles's mind. He seemed to sink farther into himself.

The receptionist picked up the phone at the doctor's office. "Mabel? This is Myrtle Clover. I'm fine, thanks. Never been in better health. But I have a good friend of mine who has a cough that needs to be looked at and I'd like Dr. Frazier to see her."

There was a pause while Myrtle listened to Mabel. Then Myrtle said, "No, she's *not* an existing patient. But she is ill and I would like her to see a doctor that I trust."

Another pause and then Myrtle said tersely, "Put Doctor Frazier on the line."

Chapter Eight

Miles's eyebrows shot up. He muttered, "Myrtle, it isn't done. The doctors have nothing to do with scheduling."

"Pooh. That's a myth. This is *his* office, and *he's* the one in charge. I'm pretty sure that he knows a good deal about what goes on with the scheduling there. It's a small town. I've no doubt that things didn't work this way when you were in *Atlanta*, but I can assure you they work this way here."

She turned her attention back to the phone. "Yes, Tommy, it's me. I know you'd rather limit the number of patients you're seeing, but this is a special case. She hasn't been to the doctor since she was a child and you'll likely never see her again unless I can persuade her to return."

Myrtle's voice had that same authoritative ring to it that it did when she was in charge of her classroom. It had always surprised Miles how people responded with alacrity to it. It was how she got most things done.

Myrtle glanced at the clock. "I most certainly *can* have her there in 45 minutes. Thanks, Tommy." She hung up looking smug.

Miles, however, looked worried. "Not to argue, Myrtle, but Wanda lives some distance away."

"I can get there and back to town in 45 minutes," said Myrtle. She made a quick phone call to Wanda to let her know she was coming. Then she pulled out her pocketbook and rifled through a fat wallet until she found her driver's license. Satisfied that she'd located it, she put it back in her purse.

Miles continued, "It's just that you don't drive very fast."

"Speed limits are there for a reason," said Myrtle as she picked up her cane and headed for the door. Miles trailed along behind her.

"Most people don't treat them as a *limit*. They're just careful to go only seven or eight miles an hour over them," said Miles.

"I'm not most people," said Myrtle with a shrug. "But I'll make sure I get there on time. The doctor is working her in."

They stepped outside and Myrtle locked the door. Then she waited for Miles to hand over his car keys. He slowly did so.

"Thank you. I'll fill you in when I get back home," said Myrtle.

Miles nodded and miserably watched as she climbed into his car, gave a jaunty little honk of the horn as a goodbye, and took off at a sedate ten miles an hour.

It took a while to reach Wanda's hubcap-covered shack. She was waiting outside in a plastic chair that had seen better days. The bony woman stood up as Myrtle approached in Miles's car.

"Done run him off, ain't we?" asked Wanda as she got into the front seat.

"Well, it was all that talk of germs, wasn't it? Miles would hardly want to go to the doctor's office after hearing that. Unless that was your intention all along? To keep him home?"

"He'd-a caught somethin' in the waiting room. Or somewhere else," said Wanda with a distracted shrug. She gave another grating, heaving cough, which made Myrtle frown.

"This is completely ridiculous. You cannot let coughs get the upper hand. Otherwise, the next thing you know, you end up with pneumonia." Myrtle clicked her tongue. She glanced over at the time and was surprised to see that there was less time to reach the doctor than she'd thought. She gently pressed the accelerator and frowned in concentration as the needle climbed up another five miles an hour.

Wanda gave her a look that was even more serious than Wanda's usual somber countenance. "Have somethin' to tell you."

"I've already gotten the message, loud and clear. I'm in danger. I now accept that this is a consistent issue in my life," said Myrtle. She glanced again at the time and then again at the speedometer in consternation. She pressed the accelerator gently and winced at the responding speed. "Don't want us to be late," she muttered. At least now she was approaching downtown Bradley.

Wanda grasped the door. "Nope. It's somethin' else. It's sad. That missing girl."

Myrtle, still very distracted with the driving, frowned. "What on earth are you talking about? What missing girl?"

"That one from long ago. That teen."

Myrtle said, "You mean the one that ran away all those years ago? Who was friends with Pearl's children?"

"Or *didn't* run away," said Wanda. "And that friendship?" She gave a descriptive shrug.

Myrtle said, "Are you saying that that girl was murdered? And that the Epps family might have something to do with it?"

She was so caught up with this new information that she didn't even notice the blue lights behind her.

Myrtle added, "Are you sure that you don't have any other information? What happened to her? Who was responsible for her death? Where her body is? Because what you've given me isn't much, Wanda."

Wanda said grimly, "Better pull over."

Myrtle gave her a narrowed sideways look. "You're not about to be sick, are you? Miles would never let me borrow his car again." She abruptly pulled over.

Wanda shook her head. "Yer bein' pulled over."

"What?" Myrtle looked in her rear-view mirror disbelievingly. "Well, this certainly takes the cake. You'd think Red would have better things to do with a murder on his hands." She rolled down her window.

Wanda gave a deep sigh that quickly turned into a cough.

Red walked up and said, "Now Miles, I don't know where you're headed . . ." He gaped at Myrtle. "Mama! What on earth are you doing?"

Myrtle gave him a prim look. "I am driving Wanda to the doctor. I'm simply trying to get there on time, which is difficult when pulled over by the police."

At this point, Wanda gave a creaking, croaking cough that turned into something more full-bodied.

Red pressed his lips together and glanced around him to make sure no one was watching. "Okay. Get her to the doctor. But slow it down and get her there in one piece."

"Naturally," said Myrtle coolly.

Wanda gave Red a crooked grin that showed off her various missing teeth before dissolving into coughing again.

Red sighed. "Let me give you a police escort, for safety's sake."

Tommy Frazier finished his quick exam of Wanda and then sat back. "You came in at a good time. You have bronchitis, but it's a hair away from being pneumonia. If you'd continued to hold off coming in, it could have been worse. I'm sure you don't want to go to the hospital."

Wanda, seeing that the doctor was waiting for a response, shook her head.

He gave her a kind look. "It's not so bad here, is it? I hope that you'll come in more frequently now. If you don't have your health, you don't have anything."

Tommy typed on his computer. "I'm going to send a prescription to your pharmacy."

Myrtle raised her eyebrows. "Under the circumstances, you should ascertain that there *is* a pharmacy."

The doctor glanced wordlessly over at Wanda, who shook her head.

He nodded. "I'll print it out and Myrtle can take you over to her drugstore."

As he was doing that, Myrtle tilted her head to one side. "It's been a while, Tommy, but if I remember correctly, you were good friends with the Epps family."

Tommy gave her a surprised look. "You have a good memory. Yes, I was friends with Boone."

"And you dated his sister, Rose?" asked Myrtle.

He sat back from his computer, eyes narrowed thoughtfully. "An *exceptionally* good memory, Miss Myrtle. That wasn't a very long relationship. We realized we were better suited to being friends."

Wanda shook her head again, this time apparently in response to Myrtle's continued involvement in a murder case. She gave a deep-throated cough.

"I suppose you've heard the news about Pearl?" asked Myrtle.

Tommy sighed. "I'm afraid so. As her physician, I was informed about her death. I was sorry to hear it. I spent a good deal of time at their house growing up."

"Do you still see Boone and Rose?" asked Myrtle. He continued looking at her curiously and she continued, "I'm simply wondering if you believe that they've changed throughout the years."

He said cautiously, "I can't speak to this as a doctor, you understand. Only as a friend. Or former friend."

"So you don't spend much time with them anymore?" asked Myrtle.

He said, "I'm afraid not. I've been very busy with work and, to be honest, they *are* different. Or maybe I'm different, I'm not sure."

Myrtle leaned in. "In what way are they different?"

Tommy pursed his mouth in thought. "Boone was always fun-loving, but there came a point where he became reckless. I know he's a prominent local businessman now, but that reckless element is still there. In my career, I can't really allow any . . . imprudent actions."

"And Rose?" asked Myrtle.

Tommy looked reluctant. "As I said, I'm not speaking as a physician. But I will say that Rose is a ghost of herself. She's just extremely delicate and fragile. I've been concerned about her, but there's not much I can do unless she comes in for a visit."

A few minutes later, Myrtle and Wanda were leaving the building with a paper prescription. Myrtle said, "We'll just run by the pharmacy and get them to fill this before I run you back home."

Wanda gazed morosely at the prescription. "Don't it take a while?"

"At the pharmacy? Not for me."

Wanda grinned her gap-toothed grin at her. "Reckon you taught the pharmacist."

"That I did," said Myrtle.

Only ten minutes later, Myrtle was driving Wanda back home with the prescription in hand.

Myrtle, now driving much more sedately, gave Wanda a sideways glance. "I thought I might just stick my head in and make sure everything is going all right at home. How is your brother?"

Wanda made a face. "Dan's same as always."

This was not welcome news. There was a reason Wanda's brother was called Crazy Dan.

Sure enough, when Myrtle pulled up to the hubcap-covered home, she saw signs that Dan had been collecting again. It didn't seem quite as bad as hoarding she'd seen on television shows, but it was messier than a regular messy house.

They walked inside the house and Myrtle's head instantly started hurting. Wanda's stuff was carefully arranged in shelving. Dan's things were stacked on the floor and piled up on surfaces. Myrtle sighed and said, "I'm sorry, Wanda. Sure does look like Dan is up to his old tricks again."

Wanda shrugged an emaciated shoulder. "Reckon it's why we can't pay the electric bill half the time. Dan likes going to the dollar store and buying stuff."

"At the dollar store?" Myrtle glanced around her.

Wanda nodded. "But even shopping at the dollar store can make a dent in yer budget if you buy this much."

Myrtle followed a path on the floor to the kitchen. There she saw the little plant that Miles had given her the last time that Wanda's house had been cleared out. Amazingly, it was blossoming here. The kitchen itself was clean, at least by Myrtle's standards. Miles may not have wanted to touch anything. And yet the relentless clutter was apparent here, too.

Myrtle said, "Will Dan be upset if we just get rid of some of this stuff?"

"Probably won't even notice. All he cares about is the buying of it," said Wanda laconically.

"I'll take a couple of bags to the Goodwill, if you can put them together. I don't want to handle a full carload, but each time I come here, I'll take some stuff away." She hesitated and looked at the prescription bottle.

"Don't worry—I'll take all the pills," said Wanda with a wink as she took out a garbage bag and started throwing things in.

"And stop reading my mind," said Myrtle in a bossy tone.

As Myrtle drove toward the Goodwill, she reflected on the fact that perhaps Wanda should have chosen better-smelling items to give away. She wasn't entirely sure what was in the bags, but they had a rather odd aroma.

Wanda had at least pointed her in an interesting direction with her remarks earlier on Tara Blanton. Myrtle frowned. She'd taught that little girl, and she bristled at the thought that it hadn't been the cut and dried runaway case that the police had apparently dismissed it as. It was a pity that Red hadn't been a cop then. And that Myrtle had been a schoolteacher instead of a sleuth. Could the Epps family really be involved? Her doctor seemed to have thought they'd changed dramatically since he'd been friends with them. Of course, who *didn't* change when you're talking about a matter of decades?

Myrtle coasted into the Goodwill to the drive-through donation lane. A vehicle was in front of her, so she rolled down the windows to let some air in . . . and some of that odd aroma out.

With the windows down, Myrtle could hear the sound of arguing. She saw the man who helped with unloading donations step back and then glance her way, eyes rolling. She listened and heard a familiar voice.

Rose Epps wailed, "You just can't give all this stuff away! I had no idea what you had in this car. You said you were just going to bring bags of clothes!"

Hubert's voice was pleading in return as he leaned against the car. "Rose, baby, you can't expect me to hold on to all this stuff. This helps with the grieving process."

"*What* grieving? All you want to do is to get rid of everything and forget about her," said Rose, voice rising to a pitch that made Myrtle wince.

"Sweetheart, listen. Sometimes it's better to just get the bad stuff over with first. Like ripping off a bandage. I would think about your mother whenever I walked past her things in the house," said Hubert, trying to sound reasonable.

"You didn't love her!" sobbed Rose. And with that, she hopped into the car and drove away, tires screeching.

Hubert watched as she disappeared, shaking his head.

The attendant gestured to Myrtle to drive up in the lane and she did. She leaned out her window and said to Hubert, "I'm sorry, I couldn't help but overhear that. Can I give you a ride home?"

He blinked in surprise when he saw her. "Myrtle! Yes, that'd be great, if you could." There was a pause while he took in the picture of Myrtle sitting behind the wheel. "Somehow, I didn't realize that you were still driving."

Myrtle drew herself up in the seat. "I'm an excellent driver."

"Is this your car, then?" He frowned at the car.

"I've borrowed it from Miles to run errands. But I'm planning on visiting Boone at his dealership very soon. I have far too many places to go. I'm constantly asking for rides or borrowing cars," said Myrtle with a sniff.

The Goodwill attendant quickly grabbed the bags while Hubert climbed into the front seat. He wrinkled his nose at the unusual odor. Then Myrtle drove away.

Hubert sighed and said, "I'm sorry you had to see that scene with Rose. She's taking this super-hard. I guess we just react to things differently. After the police were done looking for evidence and took away whatever they needed, I decided that it would help me heal if I gave away some stuff. It just constantly reminds me of Pearl, otherwise. But Rose doesn't see things that way. I don't believe she's thinking straight. What on earth would she do with Pearl's clothes? It's not like they were even the same size and they didn't wear the same styles."

"The poor girl just lost her mother. Naturally, she's having a tough time adjusting. Anyone would," said Myrtle as she headed to downtown Bradley.

Hubert sounded uncertain. "Would they? This much? You know, the bad thing is that Pearl was the one who sort of held Rose together. I love that girl and would do anything for her. But I'm not blind to the fact that she struggles."

"Struggles in what way?" Myrtle saw Red talking to another officer outside the police station. He glanced up and his eyes narrowed as he saw her driving yet another passenger. She gave him a cheery wave and a smug smile as she continued on her way.

"With life. She's always been so delicate—so frail," said Hubert.

Myrtle said, "There's no question that Rose is incredibly frail right now. But as her former teacher, I didn't see a hint of it."

Hubert gave her a patronizing smile. "That was a long time ago. Wouldn't you have forgotten?"

Myrtle snapped, "I haven't forgotten anything about teaching school."

He quickly said, "I stand corrected. I'm just saying that I'm sure that *I'd* have forgotten things from thirty years ago."

Myrtle gave him a sidelong glance. "As I recall, Rose first seemed fragile when her friend disappeared." She pulled onto Hubert's street.

Hubert said gruffly, "It was a stressful time for Rose. She kept saying that she blamed herself. Pearl and I guessed that she felt responsible for the fact that the girl ran off . . . that she should have known she was planning to do it. She and the girl were friends and had been for most of their lives. It was a very selfish thing that Tara did to both her family and her friends. Her poor parents never did get over her leaving and never heard from her again. They ended up moving out of town because everything was a reminder of their daughter."

"What if she *didn't* run away?" asked Myrtle.

Chapter Nine

Hubert stared at her. "What are you saying?"

"I'm saying, what if something happened to her?" Myrtle pulled the car into Hubert's driveway. She turned to study him. His face and neck were a mottled red.

"You mean, like an accident? Went swimming in the lake and drowned?" demanded Hubert.

"Or something else. Perhaps she met with foul play," suggested Myrtle.

Hubert gave a short, dismissive laugh. "Who would murder Tara Blanton? She was a child."

"She was fifteen. Not so much of a child," said Myrtle.

Hubert grabbed the door handle as if he were desperate to get out of the car. "I don't know exactly what you're implying, Myrtle, but if you're blaming my family for something, you're dead wrong. I wasn't even at home when that girl disappeared, and neither was Pearl. The kids didn't know a thing about it. And Rose was devastated. Now I thank you for the ride, but I need to be on my way."

And with that, he slammed the car door behind him and trotted off to the house at a fast clip.

Myrtle drove to Miles's house thoughtfully. When she pulled into the driveway, she saw that he was outside, pruning the bushes in the front of his house.

"How is Wanda?" he asked.

Myrtle noticed that he had a little plastic caddy full of cleaning supplies on his front porch. Next to them was a pair of plastic gloves. She sighed. Wanda had really done her a disservice with that ghastly horoscope.

"Wanda is fine. She has bronchitis and is on antibiotics," said Myrtle.

Miles frowned. "Bronchitis. Is that contagious?"

Myrtle sighed. "I asked Tommy, and he said hers shouldn't be. It wasn't caused by infection." She paused. "I also gave Hubert a ride. Rose had left him at the Goodwill."

"The Goodwill? What were you doing out there?" asked Miles. He took off his yardwork gloves and put on some latex gloves. Then he picked up some cleaning bottles and moved toward his car.

Myrtle scowled. "I told you it wasn't contagious."

"But maybe Hubert has something. It doesn't hurt to wipe everything down," said Miles.

Myrtle said, "Wanda's house has become overrun again by Crazy Dan's junk. I was dropping off some bags."

Miles had just sat in the car to wipe down the steering wheel and made a face. "What was in those bags?"

"That's unknown," said Myrtle impatiently. "Look, can you be quick with that? I want to go to the dealership with you to talk to Boone."

Miles scrubbed at the wheel and then sprayed Lysol around the car, centering especially around Wanda's seat. "Boone? Don't tell me you're really serious about buying a car."

"Why not? Haven't I been borrowing yours enough lately? I *could* be interested, anyway, and that's what I want Boone to think."

"And Red too, I guess," said Miles as he wiped down the dashboard with an antibacterial wipe.

"It's two for the price of one," said Myrtle.

Miles looked critically around the car. "This will have to do, I suppose."

"Good. And Boone is always the very picture of health so you won't have to fear any germs there," said Myrtle.

"I've already refilled my hand sanitizer, just to be on the safe side." Miles carefully put the used wipes in a grocery bag and then pulled off his latex gloves and tossed them in the same bag.

Myrtle watched as he put it straight into his outdoor garbage bin. She half-expected him to put up a sign with 'bio-hazard' written on it.

Boone's dealership was quite a big place. And as soon as Miles had pulled into the parking lot, a smiling salesman had immediately greeted them.

Myrtle said tersely, "We'd like to see Boone, please."

"Oh, you're a friend of Boone's?" asked the young salesman.

"Just tell him that Myrtle Clover is here, if you could."

As he obediently hurried off, Miles said, "You're throwing your weight around a lot this week."

"It just happens that I'm dealing with a lot of middle-aged former students this week," said Myrtle.

A minute later, Boone Epps came striding out to join them with a spring in his step. He reached out and gently gave Myrtle a hug. "Miss Myrtle! My favorite teacher of all time! How are you doing?"

Myrtle tried to stay serious, but couldn't help the smile that pulled the corners of her mouth up. "I wish I could say that you were one of my favorite students of all time, Boone."

He gave a big hee-hawing laugh. "But then we'd know you were lying! I gave you far too much of a hard time."

Myrtle said, "And I'm not altogether sure *you're* not lying. After all, I'm here in a customer capacity, looking at cars."

He grinned, showing off a line of perfect teeth. "Well, you've come to the right place. And I *wouldn't* lie to you to sell you a car because I'm that convinced that we have the absolute perfect car on the lot for you."

Boone suddenly stuck out his hand in Miles's direction and Miles reluctantly took it. Myrtle was sure that there would be hand sanitizer being squirted as soon as it could be done without observation.

"Hi, I'm Boone Epps. I don't think I've had the pleasure of your acquaintance."

Miles said, "Miles Bradford."

Boone snapped his fingers. "That name's so familiar to me. Wait. I've got it! One of the pilgrims, wasn't it? Are you related? That would be quite a distinguished line."

Myrtle smirked at Boone. "I'm glad I taught you English and not history. The pilgrim you're trying to come up with is Miles Standish."

Miles cleared his throat. "Or perhaps William Bradford."

Boone's eyes twinkled and he gave that hee-hawing laugh again. "I made a mash-up of two pilgrims! You sure don't do that every day. Now I know you good folks didn't want to spend the whole day yapping with me at the dealership. What can I help you with so that I can send you on your way with a wonderful new car?"

Miles, surreptitiously pulling the hand sanitizer from his khakis pocket, gave Myrtle a quelling look. He was apparently most concerned that Myrtle *would* somehow drive out of the dealership with a wonderful new car.

Myrtle beamed at Boone. "As a matter of fact, Boone, I want a wonderful *used* car. Something reasonably priced and very safe. But I'll want to test-drive a series of them to make sure they're exactly what I want. And I may not do that all today. I do get very tired sometimes and need to spread out my activities."

Miles raised his eyebrows. Myrtle was never tired. Myrtle wasn't tired even at 3 a.m. when *everyone* was tired.

"But I also wanted to tell you how very sorry I am about your mother. I had a lot of respect for Pearl," said Myrtle.

Boone grew solemn. His eyes held a glimmer of tears in them before he hastily blinked them away. "I appreciate that, Miss Myrtle. Mama had a lot of respect for *you*. Your words are high praise." He paused. "I heard that you were there right after Dad found Mama."

"Miles and I both were. You see, we had a very odd incident that happened at my house directly before we left for your parents' house," said Myrtle. "It's been worrying me."

Boone tilted his head to one side and squinted thoughtfully at her.

Myrtle continued, "Pearl had asked me yesterday morning if I could edit her memoir manuscript for her. You knew that she'd finished it?"

Boone chuckled. "I did. And boy, were we all surprised! When Mama said she'd be writing a book, I guess we all figured that it would be one of those dreams that never really gets done. But she stuck to it."

"Well, she intimated that the family might not be pleased about it. Do you have any idea why?" asked Myrtle in a stern voice.

Boone considered this. "I suppose Daddy wasn't going to be happy. He never likes being the center of attention and if Mama had written a book, maybe he thought that people were going to be oohing and ahhing over it and her."

Myrtle frowned. "I can't imagine that's a reason anyone would be unhappy about a book. Anyway, Miles and I left for lunch. When we came back from Bo's Diner, the manuscript was gone."

Boone said, "You sure about that, Miss Myrtle? If your house is anything like mine, things go missing in it from time to time. It probably just got shoved into some drawer and you only *thought* it was gone."

Miles cleared his throat. "I can attest to the fact that it was no longer in the house. It hadn't been put in a drawer. It had been stolen."

Miles seemed quite affronted by the implication that Myrtle and he had ineptly managed to misplace a large sheaf of paper.

Boone frowned. "So someone broke into your house and stole my mother's book?"

"Exactly. Someone who had something to lose. From what your mother told me, she was tired of harboring secrets. Maybe someone wasn't quite as ready to let go of them as she was," said Myrtle.

Boone raised his hands as if in surrender. "No secrets here, just great cars. That's a terrible segue, but honestly, Miss Myrtle, I don't really see how I can help you at all. I'm all torn up over Mama and it was a horrible shock, but life must go on. I figured if I came on into work then everything would feel more normal again."

"Has it helped?" asked Myrtle, looking doubtful.

"Until you showed up and started asking questions," said Boone. His voice sounded teasing, but there was a sharp edge to it. "And, like I said, I can't even help you with your questions because I have no idea what happened. I was at work all day. I didn't know anything about it until Red stopped by to let me know. And I have no idea what was in Mama's book because I never read it—I never even realized that she had actually written it."

Myrtle studied Boone. Boone shifted. It was the same look Myrtle gave when a student asked her for extra credit points on the day before the final exam. "But Pearl said the opposite when she came by my house. She said that at a family dinner the night before she died that she told everyone that she'd finished her book."

Boone reddened a little but somehow still maintained that carefree, friendly look. It must have been all those years being a car salesman. His expression didn't even look forced or faked. He raised his hands and laughed. "You got me, Miss Myrtle!

You're absolutely right. I've been so busy that I'd forgotten that Mama laid that bombshell revelation on us at supper. She enjoyed doing it, actually. She saw the shock on our faces."

Myrtle backed off a little now. She gave him a smile. "I can imagine that she felt smug about that. She clearly kept her progress on the book a secret."

Miles said, "Although the family all knew that she was planning on writing it, so it couldn't have been that much of a surprise."

Boone wagged a finger at him. "Oh, but it was. I thought it was something that Mama had just tossed out casually one day—that she planned on writing a book. I thought it was more like a bucket list item. You know: go to Paris, go skydiving, write a book."

"The problem is that the whole family forgot who they were dealing with," said Myrtle, a hint of irritation in her voice. "This wasn't someone unfamiliar with setting and meeting goals."

Boone said, "You're one-hundred percent right, Miss Myrtle. That's what we all forgot. Mama was a genius at organization. She likely set herself a word goal every day and obviously met it every single one."

Myrtle said, "She could do anything she set her mind to. I'm just stunned at Pearl's death and feel very connected to it, since she was at my house and had elicited my help. And somehow, the task that I was asked to do is tied into her death. I feel responsible, in a way. And I want to get more of a handle on what was going on in her life."

Boone sighed and considered this for a moment. "So you're going to help Red out. Well, I get it. Mama inspired that kind of devotion. Let's see if I can paint a picture of what was going on with Mama's life at home. I guess I'll start out with Rose."

Miles said, "We've seen your sister since your mother's death. She seems very rattled."

Boone snorted. "When is Rose *not* rattled?" He paused and said, almost to himself, "I'll need to go by and visit her. Maybe she's worse than usual." He frowned as if this thought concerned him more than Myrtle thought it would. But perhaps Boone was a more attentive brother than most. He and his sister had seemed to be close when they were in high school, too.

Myrtle said, "Your father seemed to think that she is very fragile."

Boone said, "The problem is that Rose needed a lot of help. I guess it was more 'emotional support.' She would call, or text, or go by my mom's house and ask her all kinds of questions and tell her about any little thing that she was worried about or that was on her mind. I can't even tell you the number of hours that my mother must have spent trying to talk Rose off the cliff." He looked at Myrtle and Miles and grinned. "Figuratively speaking, of course."

Miles said, "Well, there aren't that many cliffs around here."

"I don't remember her being that way her whole life," said Myrtle, scowling.

Boone shook his head. "Here I'll have to correct you. She *has* been that way for decades. She cries at the drop of a hat, too."

"I don't remember Rose being that way when she was a teen, though. Not when she was my student. Although, as I seem to recall, she started acting more fearful and anxious around the time that her friend disappeared," said Myrtle, watching Boone closely.

Boone's smile froze for a few seconds before he said, "That's only natural; right, Miss Myrtle? After all, Tara was Rose's best friend. In fact, Tara served as Rose's confidant before my mother did. Makes sense, doesn't it? Usually teen girls prefer to confide in their peers instead of a parent. So Rose lost a lot when Tara ran away."

"Does Rose get along with your father well?" asked Myrtle.

Boone snorted. "Daddy isn't the gruff guy that he usually is whenever Rose is around. He's real protective of her. Too protective. That's part of the reason Rose is the nervous Nelly that she is—because he coddles her so much."

"And your mother and you? Did your father act the same around you?" asked Miles curiously.

"Not at all. He's been downright rude to both of us, when it suited him. Not that he wasn't also supportive," said Boone quickly. But his tone made Myrtle think it might not be true. Boone continued in a rough voice, "I don't think anybody could have done this. I still would rather think my mother had a terrible accident on those stairs. She could get distracted from time to time and she always had a lot on her mind. Mama had stumbled on those very stairs many times in the past and I feel like this time she just couldn't catch herself." Boone took a deep breath and blew it back out again in puffs. "But if it's not an accident, I reckon I'd have to say that it was Edward who was responsible."

Myrtle and Miles frowned at each other.

Miles said, "This is a new name for us. There's an Edward in the family?"

Boone gave a harsh laugh. "No, but I bet he'd sure want to be. Y'all know him, I'm sure. Edward Hammond is his name."

Chapter Ten

Miles made a grunt of recognition. "Edward. Yes, I've played Scrabble with him before."

Boone laughed. "Is that what y'all are doing for entertainment around Bradley? I'll have to introduce you to some better hangouts. Joe's Bar has a dollar menu on Thursday nights."

Miles's face reflected great concern that Boone might somehow induce him to go to a bar for dollar items.

Myrtle said briskly, "Back to Edward Hammond. I'm confused as to what role he plays in your family. Is he a cousin?"

Boone raised his eyebrows. "He's Nell's beau."

Myrtle and Miles exchanged a look again.

Miles said carefully, "Nell Prentiss?"

Boone said, "Yep! My aunt."

Myrtle frowned. "But your aunt has never married. And I've not heard of her being in a relationship. Besides, Edward has been married for decades."

Boone wagged a finger her way. "Nell might be an old maid, but that doesn't mean that she hasn't had a beau. And Edward *was* married for decades. They've been separated for a while. Edward has his own place."

Myrtle said slowly, "That's very surprising news. I hadn't heard anything about it."

Boone said, "That's because they've been able to keep it on the down-low." He stood back and grinned at them with the expression of someone who knows they're delivering a bombshell.

Myrtle said, "What makes you think that Edward would kill Nell's sister? That doesn't sound like a very reasonable thing to do if you're trying to get in good with the family."

Boone shrugged. "At that family dinner you're talking about, Edward got pretty upset. He stormed out and Nell left to follow him out. I reckon he didn't want his relationship with Nell to be revealed in Mama's book. Nell is prim and proper. She wouldn't want anything to appear untoward. Although I'm pretty sure that Nell being Nell, there *wasn't* anything untoward."

"You think her relationship with Edward was in your mother's memoir?" Miles pushed his glasses up farther on his nose and blinked at Boone.

"Sure. She said that she put everything in there and didn't leave anything out. That should include her sister and Edward, too." Now Boone looked uneasy. "I'm not saying he *did* it, mind you. But I sure can't think of anybody else who would have. He isn't family after all."

Boone now had that restless look about him that Myrtle remembered from when he was in school. It meant that his limited attention span had just about hit its end. She quickly changed tack. "How about if you show me one of your used cars? Then I can take it for a spin. I'll bring it right back, of course."

The tension in Boone's shoulders seemed to relax a little, and he grinned at her. "No worries, Miss Myrtle. I know where you live, remember? You can keep it out the rest of the day or even return it tomorrow if you want. All I want is for you to be happy with whatever car you end up with. Then we can repeat the process a few more times with different vehicles so that you can make sure you've got the best one for you."

Miles was giving Myrtle another one of those sideway looks, but Myrtle studiously ignored him. "That's perfect, Boone. Lead the way."

Just thirty minutes later, Myrtle was driving a bright red sedan out of the dealership. She followed Miles home for Miles to drop off his car. Then Miles reluctantly got into Myrtle's loaner. She backed out of Miles's driveway. Miles grasped the door with white knuckles.

Myrtle gave him a cross look. "I'm an excellent driver, Miles."

"Well, I'm a nervous passenger."

Myrtle said, "Moving on, let's consider what we've found out so far."

"We've found out that Pearl's family is very odd," said Miles. "Even Boone. Right now, he gets the prize for normalcy and I don't think he's even all that normal."

Myrtle entered downtown Bradley. She spotted Red's police car ahead and gave a jaunty toot of her horn that nearly made Miles jump through the windshield. Red glowered at her as she waved and smugly drove on.

"All families are odd," said Myrtle with a shrug.

Miles, having observed her interaction with Red, said, "That's true."

"But not every family houses a killer," said Myrtle thoughtfully.

"Perhaps it's as Boone said—not a family member at all, but a friend. Like Edward. It sounded like Pearl was ready to expose his secrets, too," said Miles.

Myrtle slowed the car down even more as they approached downtown. "Edward seemed to consider himself practically a family member, though, so that doesn't really count. Edward should be the next one on our list to speak to."

Miles said, "How do you propose to do that? He's retired, isn't he? I don't think we can legitimately go knocking on his door to interrogate him about his secrets and Pearl's death."

"Well, of *course* we won't do that! We're not police officers. Fortunately, Edward's routine is something of a known entity. He's one of the old boys who likes to hang out in front of Bo's Diner with a coffee," said Myrtle. "And my stomach's growling anyway, so we might as well pick up some food. I'm craving that new menu item."

Miles made a face. "What was it again?"

"A pimento cheese dog with barbeque sauce," said Myrtle. "And it's perfection."

"Perfection for inducing indigestion," muttered Miles. He winced as Myrtle swung into a parking space outside the diner without braking until the last second. Once she stopped, he hastily got out of the car.

Sure enough, Edward Hammond was sitting on the bench outside the diner. He appeared to be almost holding court there, greeting people as they came and went while he sipped on a coffee. He was a big man with a gray handlebar mustache and a no-nonsense air.

Miles murmured, "So, are we just going to plop down next to him and start shooting questions?"

"Certainly not," said Myrtle, frowning at him. "For one thing, we need to get some food. For another, Edward's always been a bit prickly. He's not particularly fond of me."

"That can happen when a prickly person encounters someone very plain-spoken," observed Miles pointedly.

Myrtle pressed her lips together. Then she smiled. "I have an idea."

"Have you eaten yet?" called out Myrtle as she approached Edward, thumping her cane on the pavement as she walked.

"Eaten?" Edward looked suspiciously at Myrtle. "I have, yes, but it was a long while back."

"Why don't you join Miles and me? We'd love the company," said Myrtle.

Miles looked as though he wasn't sure that was the case, but he gave Edward a tight smile.

"Well, okay. Haven't seen either one of you for a while," said Edward.

Myrtle beamed at him. "I know. I was just telling Miles how it would be good to catch up with you, and here you are!"

Fortunately, the diner wasn't crowded. Usually when they arrived, there was a wait and no place to sit. But this was a be-tween-meals time and the place was a lot quieter. Myrtle pur-posely steered the waitress who seated them to a quiet booth in the back. Miles squirted his hands with sanitizer.

Myrtle ordered the new pimento cheese and barbeque sauce dog. Miles ordered a side salad with the ranch dressing on the side. Edward, on the other hand, went all out and ordered a double-decker hamburger with sides of baked beans, potato salad, and a slice of lemon pie.

Myrtle, not wanting to be stuck with Edward's bill, told the waitress, "Individual checks, please."

Miles hid a smile.

Myrtle leaned forward and gave Edward a sympathetic look. "I hope you're doing well, Edward. It *has* been a while."

Edward sighed. "Well, I suppose I've been doing all right. But you know how it is. My sciatica will act up. And I've had another cataract that I need to take care of. Not to mention the fact that I'm having a harder time getting around than I used to."

Myrtle pursed her lips. She did not want this to be an ordinary conversation with a fellow senior. That's because most ordinary conversations with her peers descended into healthcare issues rapidly. They all had war stories about their doctor visits. In fact, Myrtle was sure she'd had a lucky escape when Miles demonstrated the voice recorder for his latest conversation with his physician. She tried redirecting. "I know what you mean. But I was really referring to all the recent troubles at the Epps house. I just found out how close you are to the family."

Edward's face grew thunderous. He hissed, "That is *not* for public consumption! You newspaper reporters are all the same. Get a guy off his guard and then delve into his private life. Put it all over the papers."

Miles said mildly, "Edward, I don't know if you're reading the same paper I am. The *Bradley Bugle* focuses on little league scores and stories like Jim Reed's complete collection of National Geographic Magazines. It's not a gossip rag."

Myrtle sniffed. "As if I would write for a tabloid, anyway."

Edward was not quite placated and still very much on his guard. "Then I guess you found out about it when Pearl took that stupid manuscript of hers over to your house. Did you read it?"

"Considering it was in my house for less than an hour, no I *didn't* read it. But I found out from an Epps family member, whose name will go unspoken, that you had a relationship with Nell," said Myrtle.

Edward swung his head around to ensure that Myrtle hadn't been overheard. "Be quiet!" he told her. "Keep your voice down."

Myrtle said, "I also heard that you were divorced. Even in a small town like Bradley, there isn't a scandal when a divorced man dates a single lady."

Edward shifted uncomfortably. "I'm not quite divorced yet."

"Well, separated then. Whatever. I don't know what you're going on about, Edward. I was going to congratulate you on having the good sense to start seeing someone as sensible as Nell," said Myrtle huffily.

Miles looked thoughtfully at Edward. "Perhaps you're trying to protect Nell's reputation?"

Edward gave him a grateful look. "Yes. Yes, that's it exactly. Nell doesn't need to be mixed up in any kind of local gossip. And the fact that the divorce hasn't gone through yet means that tongues will wag. You don't know what my marriage was like. *She* was the one who essentially walked away from our marriage.

She was absent emotionally and quite frequently physically absent, too, since she'd travel to see her family a lot. Before long, we were separated. And that's when Nell and I started spending a little time together."

He shut his mouth quickly as the food was delivered to the table. Then, when the waitress walked safely out of earshot, he added, "But that's not the town of Bradley's business. They are in no position to judge Nell or me."

Miles, who was in the process of lifting some of his side salad to his mouth, stared at Edward's hostile tone.

Myrtle finished a bite of her hot dog and said, "It sounds like you're really passionate about that."

"Of course I am! You know what this town is like when it finds out a secret. They eat that person alive," said Edward.

Myrtle gave him a stern look. "The good people of Bradley are *not* zombies, Edward. But I do find it very interesting that you're so wound up about the word getting out. I heard that you walked away from the dinner table when Pearl announced that she'd finished her memoir and was sending it to me to edit."

Edward flushed again. "You're saying that I was so upset about the book that I killed Pearl over it."

"I believe *you* just said that," said Myrtle.

Edward seemed to be trying to contain his temper. He took another bite of his meal and chewed it thoughtfully. Finally, he said, "All right; I was mad. I had no idea that Pearl would take writing that memoir seriously. Then she springs it on us at dinner. You can imagine how we all felt."

Myrtle said, "I can't quite imagine that, no. That's why I need your help."

Edward said, "It was quite the bombshell. Boone gave one of those horsey laughs of his to hide his panic. Rose started weeping, which is totally normal for her, of course. Hubert looked annoyed. And Nell, bless her, turned completely pale. That's what got me so keyed up—seeing how upset she was by the news."

Miles cleared his throat. "I don't understand why this was such a shock to everyone. Didn't the family see her typing some days? Or a *lot* of days? It would have taken some time to write a book that long."

Edward shrugged. "After she initially told us that she was writing a memoir, she didn't say anything else about it. I thought it was some flight of fancy that Pearl had had. As far as typing, Pearl was always sending emails to committee members. You know how involved she was in everything."

Miles said, "That's what's confusing to me. Pearl was so involved and so well-respected in this town. Why would she do something to jeopardize her standing? Why would she write something that would make people think less of her?"

Edward shrugged. "You'd have to ask Pearl that, and she's not available." He glowered at Myrtle. "But I had nothing to do with her death. I was with my wife then."

"You're still doing things together?" asked Myrtle.

"Nope. I was there trying to convince her that we needed to proceed with a divorce," said Edward.

Myrtle said, "So you were with your wife, working out details. You don't know anything about the missing manuscript at my house."

Edward stiffened. "I'm not in the habit of breaking into elderly women's houses."

Myrtle glared at him. "From where I'm sitting, we're both elderly, Edward."

"There you go. Can you see me clamoring into somebody's window to grab some pile of papers?" Edward sighed. "As much as I hate to say it, Rose is the most unstable one of the bunch. And now she's even *more* unstable, from what I can see. At that family dinner that you're referring to? After Pearl made her announcement about the book, Rose whispered, "It's all my fault."

"Her fault? What did she mean by that?" asked Myrtle.

"Who knows? It's sort of been her mantra for decades. Hubert shut Rose up real quick at dinner so she wouldn't say anything else. The man is very protective of her. I thought Rose had some sort of martyr syndrome, but Nell has always felt that Rose takes everything too personally. That she has some kind of guilt complex or something."

"But we understood that Rose depended on her mother to be her confidant," said Miles. "Why would she do anything to endanger that?"

Edward shrugged and finished chewing a large mouthful of food. "That doesn't mean that she wouldn't turn on her. I'm not saying that Rose would plan some kind of elaborate plot to murder her mother. But would she become frustrated or upset in some petty way and shove her? It's certainly possible."

Miles said, "So you're thinking that the whole thing could have been a tragic accident. That Rose could have merely given her a little push and not ever even intended for her mother to fall down the stairs."

"It's certainly possible. Then she may have panicked and took off out of the house," said Edward.

Myrtle said, "And then had the presence of mind to break into my home and steal her mother's manuscript?"

Edward sighed. "I don't really see her doing that. But Rose could have persuaded Boone to. Boone is up for anything and he and his sister have always been close. At least, he worries a lot about her."

Myrtle looked regretfully at her empty plate. Her pimento cheese and barbeque dog and sides were already gone and she'd been so absorbed in the conversation that she hadn't even had a chance to enjoy them. Irritated, she shifted her questions to Nell in retaliation. "What was Nell's relationship with her sister like?"

Edward blinked. "With Pearl? It was fine. Everyone got along with Pearl because she was so easy-going."

"And Nell isn't?" guessed Miles.

Myrtle shot him a look. Every once in a while, Miles seemed to step out of his sidekick status and into full-blown investigator mode. She had to remind him of his place.

"Nell isn't like Pearl. She's not difficult to get along with, but she's not the Queen Bee like Pearl was," said Edward.

Myrtle said, "Although Nell is involved in groups, just like Pearl was."

Edward said, "Well, she really enjoys the bellringing at the church. And she'll play Scrabble now and then, as I think Miles does."

"I'm a sub," said Miles. Miles had no desire to play Scrabble more than he already did.

"But Nell isn't nearly as involved in things as Pearl was. Pearl was in everything and she was in charge of everything. Nell is a bit quieter and prefers not to be out of the house the entire day," said Edward.

Myrtle said, "So they were different. And you're saying that they did get along, on the basis of the fact that Pearl was easy to get along with?"

Edward finished his food and pushed his plate away impatiently. "It wasn't just for that reason. They were sisters. They've lived in the same town for their entire lives and they're invested in each other. Even though Nell disagreed with Pearl sometimes, she always supported her."

"Disagreed with Pearl how?" asked Myrtle.

Edward said, "Nell was very protective of her little sister. Sometimes she felt that Pearl wasn't taking care of herself. She wasn't crazy about how Hubert treated Pearl, for one. That could lead to disagreements because Pearl would stand up for Hubert and Nell would roll her eyes over that."

Myrtle raised her eyebrows. "Pearl and Hubert had a challenging relationship? I'm not sure that I was aware of that. Every time that Pearl spoke of Hubert, she always had a funny story to tell. She seemed quite fond of him."

"Strangely, she was. Even though Hubert did absolutely nothing to help her out and sat around drinking way too much. Nell would fuss about that most of all. Pearl would have volunteering and committee meetings all day long and then she'd come home to find that Hubert was sacked out on the sofa in front of the TV with a bunch of empty beer cans around. The house would be a mess and he'd have made himself snacks and not even put away the food." Edward shook his head. "And after all that, Hubert didn't even show Pearl any respect. I guess she was just used to it, but it wasn't right."

Miles said, "He wasn't actually abusive, though, right—or was he?"

Edward said, "Well, he wasn't kind. Pearl would be all gussied up for a Christmas party or some other occasion and Hubert would hoot about the fact that Pearl wasn't a fashion model. He just wasn't much of a husband and Nell would tell Pearl to leave him and to live with her. But Pearl would stand up for Hubert."

Miles said, "Your first instinct was that *Rose* would be the most likely suspect in her mother's death. But could Hubert have shoved Pearl down the stairs?"

Edward immediately shook his head. "Hubert isn't a physical man. Like I said, his normal pose is slouching on a sofa in front of a television. I can't see him acting out that way." He picked up his check. "Now, if y'all will excuse me, I have some stuff that I need to do. Thanks for eating with me." The last was said in an uncertain tone as if the lunch hadn't been exactly what he'd expected.

Myrtle frowned at him as he walked away. "He sure is throwing suspicion on everyone but himself. And yet he's the only one who we've heard was angry when Pearl announced that the book was finished. There's more to that story."

Miles said dryly, "Well, unless we're going to run after him and interrogate him, our conversation is over with."

Myrtle snorted. "He said he had 'stuff' he needed to do. I bet when we leave he'll be camped out again on that bench out front with a fresh coffee."

"Regardless, he's done with us for now. And I'd like to get out of here, myself. There are more people coming in, which means a whole fresh assortment of germs." Miles was gazing at the door with concern as a large family with several children came in.

They paid their bills and walked out of the diner. Sure enough, Edward was sitting on the bench, talking to a couple of old men.

"Typical," hissed Myrtle as they climbed into the car.

Chapter Eleven

Miles said in a hopeful voice, "You're dropping me off at home, right?"

"But I'm having such a good time driving! I feel like there's more work I can do on this case, too."

Miles said, "We've spoken to everyone, Myrtle. Everyone who's associated with the family has told us where they were, their relationship with Pearl, and who they think might have killed her. We've earned the opportunity to rest for a while."

Myrtle snapped her fingers. "I just thought of something. We should go to the newspaper office and read up on the old papers from when Tara Blanton disappeared. Maybe that will help jog my memory."

"Why can't we just go home and read up on it online?" asked Miles.

Myrtle said, "Do you really believe that Sloan Jones has scanned all of those old papers and made them available online? You wildly overestimate his work ethic. Speaking of, considering what I saw yesterday, I should make sure that he's working on tomorrow's edition."

Miles said, "You mean he hasn't had a student intern scan old papers? Or a part-time worker? All of that stuff should surely be online by now."

"Welcome to Bradley," said Myrtle with a sniff.

Myrtle drove the very short distance to the newspaper office and parked in front. When she and Miles walked in, Sloan was so deep in thought that he didn't even react.

"He's in a bad way," murmured Miles. "He wasn't even startled when you walked in. He *always* jumps when he sees you."

They walked over closer to Sloan, who was at the far end of the dimly lit newsroom.

Myrtle said crisply, "Are you all right? I feel the sudden need to follow up and make sure that the next edition of the newspaper is ready to go to press."

Sloan nodded. "It's ready. Don't worry—you made your point last time. And you're absolutely right that the readers should get their newspaper every day."

Myrtle said, "Well, that *is* a relief since I don't really have the energy right now to produce an entire newspaper with you at the end of the day today. But I do need something from you . . . some back issues of the paper."

Sloan nodded his head toward a mass of papers in a haphazard stack on a shelf. "Those are from the last two months."

"No, I mean *real* back issues, from when you were in high school and weren't working here. Where would those be?" asked Myrtle.

Sloan said, "Those will be on microfiche, Miss Myrtle. Sure you want to go back that far?" He sounded hopeful that she would give up and leave the newsroom altogether so that he could be alone with his melancholy again.

"Where is the microfiche reader?" asked Myrtle, narrowing her eyes as she surveyed the chaos of the newsroom.

Sloan sighed as if he carried the weight of the world on his shoulders. He stood up and unerringly walked to a back corner of the newsroom. Somehow, although this space was always the picture of pandemonium, Sloan always seemed to know where everything was. You could ask him for a printed photo from ten years ago and he'd go right to a teetering stack and find it buried within.

Sloan proceeded to excavate a heap of old equipment—computer monitors from the eighties, desktops from the nineties—and pull out a contraption old enough to make the ancient computers look relevant. "Here you go." He carried it over to a table, shoved aside papers and a box containing pens, rubber bands, and paper clips and plugged in the machine.

"Remember how to work one of these beauties?" asked Sloan in the tone of someone who really didn't want to provide instruction.

"I can figure it out. I've used microfiche before," said Myrtle. Decades ago, but still.

Miles said, "Where are the archived newspapers on microfiche?"

Sloan showed them a cabinet, also obscured by old technology, that had deep drawers containing boxes of dated film. "You should find everything here," he said. Although he sounded rather doubtful. He walked back to the other side of the newsroom to continue whatever it was that he'd been doing.

Myrtle and Miles spent the next fifteen minutes figuring out the filing system for the archived stories and finding the year they were looking for.

Myrtle fiddled with the microfiche reader for about fifteen minutes more until she found the headline she was looking for. "Here we are," she breathed.

Myrtle and Miles were silent for a while as they read the story. Myrtle sat back and shook her head. "What a terrible time."

Miles said, "Well, at least we have a date and some more information." He glanced over at Sloan, slumped over the desk. "Would he mind if I used some of his paper and a pen to jot down notes?"

"Heavens, no!" said Myrtle with a snort. "Look at this place. You could bring in a forklift and remove paper and pens and he'd never even notice. In fact, a forklift is probably what this room needs."

Miles carefully chose a notebook and a pen from a nearby desk and wrote the date of Tara Blanton's disappearance. "This is all new to me," he murmured.

"It's been so long that it's almost as if I'm reading about it for the first time, myself. What are you writing?" asked Myrtle.

Miles cleared his throat. "That Tara Blanton, aged 15, was an active and popular girl at her school. That she was a good student and cared about her grades."

Myrtle nodded. "That's all true. She was a cheerleader and an academic, to boot. That's what struck me as so odd. Runaways aren't ordinarily girls who have lots of friends and are conscientious about grades and showing up for their activities.

Everyone just assumed that she'd left home because murder just didn't happen in Bradley."

Miles raised his eyebrows. "From what I've seen, it happens fairly regularly." He glanced back again at the old article and then said, "She left her house one afternoon and didn't return. But the paper points out that she didn't take a suitcase or anything with her."

Myrtle said, "As I recall, they thought she might have had an accident. They did search the lake."

Miles nodded. "Which the story mentions. But it also raises the question of why she would have even been at the lake. It wasn't a nice day, and it was wintertime. She wasn't wearing a swimsuit and hadn't told anyone that she had plans to swim or go boating."

Myrtle nodded. "I'd always wondered exactly *how* she would have run away. She was only fifteen years old. She couldn't drive a car by herself and even if she could, her parents' cars were still at their house."

"Bus?" asked Miles.

"The nearest bus stop is in the next town over," said Myrtle.

Miles said, "Maybe one of her friends gave her a lift to the bus stop?"

Myrtle said, "She would have had friends who could drive. But I find it hard to believe that one of them would drive her to the bus stop, drop her off, and then never give the police or her family any information about Tara's whereabouts. I mean, her parents were *frantic*. I can't imagine that a teenager would want them to be that way when they knew she was safe."

Miles said, "But maybe they were scared to give information. Maybe they thought they'd get into trouble. These were teens, so they might not have been thinking all that clearly."

Myrtle shrugged. "But those kids were all very tight. It was a very loyal friend group. I just don't see it."

"Maybe she hitched a ride?"

Myrtle made a face. "No one really hitchhiked back then. No, I think Wanda's right."

Miles frowned. "Wanda said something about it?"

"Oh, that's right; you weren't there. Wanda said Tara Blanton didn't run away. The implication is that she was murdered," said Myrtle.

Miles looked agitated . . . either because of the possibility of yet another victim or because the mention of Wanda had reminded him of her prediction for him (that he had somehow forgotten since he arrived at the newsroom). "Aren't you going to let Red know?"

"I've already mentioned Tara Blanton to Red, mostly because he knew her growing up. They are all the same age. But can you see me telling Red that Wanda the psychic says that the girl never left town? He'd probably think that Wanda was somehow either involved in her disappearance or that she knew something about it," said Myrtle.

"And you don't think she does?" asked Miles.

"Not like Red suspects. Wanda wasn't at school with them. She would never have known Tara. Anything that Wanda knows, it's because of her . . . talent." Myrtle was aware that Miles started getting uncomfortable if the conversation veered too much into Wanda's unusual gift.

Miles looked at the article one more time. "It says that some neighbors and other residents were questioned but no one had any information. And that the Blanton family claimed that they'd not had any sort of argument or disagreement with Tara before her disappearance."

"They must have spoken to the Epps family when they were asking questions. Tara was always over at that house to see Rose," said Myrtle. She removed the microfiche film and turned off the reader. "That's probably all we'll get from the paper. After all, it was the lack of information that made the police assume Tara had run away." She called out to Sloan as they headed to the door, "I'll have another news story about the Epps murder soon."

Sloan raised a hand in response and then continued gazing morosely at his phone.

Myrtle grumbled as she and Miles walked out the door, "We're going to have to do something about Sloan. Maybe I can help find him someone else to date." She brightened. "I suppose there's always Rose."

Miles knit his brows. "I certainly hope you're talking about *another* Rose. A Rose who isn't an emotional disaster and a suspect in a murder inquiry."

Myrtle said, "Oh, she's not that bad. She simply needs someone to distract her."

"Distract her from what?" asked Miles.

"Life in general," said Myrtle with a shrug. "She needs a better companion than all of those dogs, cute as they are."

Miles said, "Let's put that off until we figure out what's going on with the Epps family. Apart from the gratuitous matchmaking, what are our plans next?"

"I want to get back home and feed Pasha. She's probably waiting on the front step now and I couldn't leave the windows open because Red would have had a hissy fit. But tomorrow morning, we should see Nell again," said Myrtle.

Miles held onto the door as Myrtle drove off. "Don't you need to drop this car off at the dealership? I could follow you over there."

"Nope! Boone doesn't care—he just wants to sell the car. I'll park it at home tonight and then we can go by the dealership and trade it out for another vehicle tomorrow." Myrtle had a smug smile on her face. "Red's brain will be boggled when I park different cars in my driveway every night."

"Getting back to Nell. How are we supposed to make this visit a natural thing?" asked Miles.

Myrtle pulled into his driveway. "Easy. I'll go back to collect my cassoulet dish."

"But it'll have only been 24 hours, Myrtle. She may not even have eaten the thing yet," said Miles.

Myrtle shrugged. "Then maybe she'll feel awkward about that. That's not really my problem."

"Or maybe she'll think you're a little crazy and pushy," suggested Miles.

"That will be her own misguided issue, then. At any rate, I have a real excuse. But let's get there early," said Myrtle.

Miles said, "Sure. That way we can wake her up as well as force her to clean out a full dish."

"I merely want to get more information on her relationship with Edward and if she thinks he lost his temper and shoved her sister," said Myrtle with a sniff. "You're acting as if I'm doing some horrible thing when I'm only trying to help *Nell* by finding out what happened to her sister."

"Right," said Miles with an eye roll. "Okay, well let me know when you're ready to head out tomorrow."

"I'll text you," said Myrtle.

After feeding Pasha, who was indeed at her door and looking reproachfully at her when she arrived, Myrtle surprised herself by actually falling asleep and sleeping through the entire night. Usually there would be ordinary, regular noises that would disturb her slumber: a dripping faucet somewhere or a dog barking at intervals outside, or even the air conditioning turning on and off. But on that particular night, she slept like the proverbial dead.

When the morning light came through her window, it startled her enough to wake her up fully. "What on earth?" muttered Myrtle. She wasn't sure when she'd last slept through the night. Maybe when she'd been a teen.

She texted Miles and got no response. "For heaven's sake," she hissed. It certainly wasn't the break of dawn.

Myrtle finished getting ready and then looked for ways to kill time while she waited. She ended up attacking her junk drawer in her kitchen. She found that she had way more junk in the drawer than she'd remembered. Apparently, anything that she'd come across that she wasn't sure exactly what its purpose was, she'd flung into the drawer to deal with later.

Finally, her phone rang. "Hello? Miles?" she asked impatiently. She glanced at the mess on her counter from the junk drawer. She'd just have to address it later.

There was a sigh from the other end. "At some point yesterday, I must have encountered a germ. I don't feel so hot, Myrtle."

Myrtle frowned. "What are your symptoms?"

There was a pause. Then he said, "Malaise."

"That sounds less like a symptom and more like you just don't want to get out of bed this morning," said Myrtle suspiciously.

Miles said, "There may be other symptoms too that just haven't manifested themselves yet."

"Well, let's not give them a chance to. We'll head on out and get our stuff done and you'll be so busy that you'll forget all about your malaise," said Myrtle briskly. "We won't be gone too long."

Forty-five minutes later, a rather sullen Miles showed up at Myrtle's door. "All set?" asked Myrtle. "Let's head on over."

Then it was just a few minutes more when Myrtle knocked on Nell's door. There was no answer.

Miles said, "Perhaps she's sleeping. People do that sometimes."

Myrtle ignored the sarcasm. "But I don't think Nell does; at least not all that much. Her car is here." She pressed on the doorbell.

"Maybe the doorbell doesn't work," suggested Miles.

"But then she'd surely hear the pounding on the door," said Myrtle.

Miles sighed. "The poor woman could be in the shower or something. Come on, Myrtle. Let's just try again later. Maybe next time we can call before we come."

But Myrtle was shaking her head. "I'm not getting a good feeling about this." She reached out and turned the doorknob. The door opened.

Miles balked. "We shouldn't go in. She's not expecting us and it's still rather early."

"It's nine o'clock! Practically the middle of the day. I'm going to check on Nell," said Myrtle.

Miles hovered on the doorstep as Myrtle pushed the door and walked into the house. "I'm hanging back here. I have no intention of catching Nell in a state of dishabille."

Myrtle ignored him. "Nell!" she bellowed. "Nell, it's Myrtle Clover! I'm here for my cassoulet dish!" She turned around. "You're safe, Miles. Nell may be many things, but she isn't deaf."

Miles reluctantly entered the darkness of Nell's front room. Myrtle was already heading deeper into the house. "Nell!"

Then there was a long pause.

Miles said, "Everything okay, Myrtle?"

Myrtle reappeared, looking grim. "Everything is *not* okay. Nell was strangled with her own scarf."

Chapter Twelve

Not ten minutes later, Red was glowering at her. "You need to stop getting involved in this mess, Mama."

Myrtle put her hands on her hips. "*Involved* in it? All Miles and I were doing was coming by for my cassoulet dish."

Miles gave Red a miserable look.

Red said, "You gave Nell a cassoulet? We'd better have the coroner double-check the cause of death then."

Myrtle glowered at him.

"And what's going on with the red car at your house? Don't tell me you've gone ahead and purchased a vehicle."

Myrtle said primly, "Boone has been very helpful. He wants to make sure I love whatever car I pick out from him so he's letting me take them home and try them out."

Red said, "Well, I'm too busy to handle that nonsense today. But we'll have a conversation about this, later. Now I've got to figure out what's happened to poor Nell."

Myrtle gave him an insincere smile and Red stomped away.

Myrtle squinted as a car pulled up. "Oh, look! It's Lieutenant Perkins with the state police. Maybe he can be a bit more helpful than Red."

Lieutenant Perkins got out of his car and gave Myrtle a smile as he walked up to her. He was a rather stern-looking man with a military haircut and very good posture. Sometimes, however, Myrtle could make him loosen up enough to provide her with information. Fortunately, Red was busy speaking with some other policemen. He was never much of a fan of Perkins and Myrtle conferring with each other.

"Lieutenant Perkins!" said Myrtle, giving him a hug. She loved giving the policeman hugs. It always surprised him and Myrtle liked it when Perkins was a little off-balance—it meant that she might be able to squeeze more information from him.

"Mrs. Clover," he said, patting her on the back awkwardly as she hugged him. "Good to see you, despite the circumstances. I understand that you and Mr. Bradford discovered Ms. Prentiss?"

Myrtle said, "That is correct. It's just terrible. I certainly hope that the police can find out what happened to poor Nell." Naturally, she believed that they *wouldn't*, and that she and Miles would end up slightly ahead of the police.

Perkins asked Myrtle a few questions, nodding seriously and taking notes from time to time. Then he nodded. "This is all very helpful, Mrs. Clover. I appreciate your thoughts on this." He seemed to be about to head on his way.

Miles cleared his throat. "When does it look like she might have been . . . well, might have passed away?"

"You make it sound so peaceful, Miles," said Myrtle. She pursed her lips. Although it was good that he was able to think of a good question to ask before they lost Perkins altogether.

Perkins said, "From what I heard reported on the way over, Ms. Prentiss would have died sometime yesterday evening. Right before dark, I'd imagine. Apparently, it's been a little while. If you'll excuse me?"

Since it didn't appear they'd be getting anything else useful at Nell's house, Myrtle and Miles walked back home.

Myrtle said, "Now we've got a full day on our plates."

Miles said archly, "Yes, we do. But I have the feeling that something has escaped your notice."

Myrtle frowned. "What's that? You mean the dealership? Boone doesn't care when I return the car."

Miles sighed. "Now I'm wondering if you even read the book."

Myrtle gaped at him. "Not book club."

"Book club. I even mentioned it to you in passing yesterday," said Miles.

"Clearly, I was contemplating Pearl's death or something equally important." Myrtle paused. "All right, I'll admit it—I remember nothing about any of it. Who's hosting? What's the title of the book? Obviously, I didn't read it."

Miles frowned. "You really weren't paying attention. Tippy picked the book because it was her month."

Myrtle snorted. "Great. Then we've ended up with some horrible novel that she claims she spots symbolism and other literary devices in."

"That's true. It's *A Long Time in Coming,*" said Miles.

Myrtle said, "Let me guess. It's about a woman who is recently divorced and endured another major life change: either the loss of her mother or the loss of her career. Now she's groundless and looking for meaning. And middle-aged."

Miles said, "I thought you said you hadn't read the book."

"I haven't. But that's the type of book that Tippy *always* picks. She's completely predictable. What's more I can tell you it's probably set at the beach or the book's action ends up at the beach while the character is finding herself. Tippy, of course, will find all sorts of hidden meaning that simply isn't there. She'll say the character is named 'Dawn' because she's experiencing the dawn of a new day." Myrtle's tone indicated exactly what she thought of this sort of analysis.

Miles said, "Actually, Tippy *won't* say those things."

"Unless Tippy has a bad case of laryngitis, she's *sure* to say those things," said Myrtle. She unlocked her front door.

Miles followed her in. "She won't because she isn't able to attend the meeting. She had to go out of town to check on her mother."

"But if Tippy picked the book, then she must be hosting." Myrtle tossed her pocketbook at the chair and missed. She made a face as things spilled out, willy-nilly.

Miles stooped and shoved the things back into her bag. "She asked me to host for her."

Myrtle said, "Oh, *wow*. And when you host, you usually spend the entire day of book club obsessing over everything. I can't believe you're even here and not at home."

"I couldn't sleep well last night, so spent half the night cleaning and organizing for the club meeting. I already have chairs, plates, and glasses set out. I've purchased the hors d'oeuvres and they're ready to be placed on the table. And right now,

I have Puddin over there putting the finishing touches on the house," said Miles.

"Oh, she'll put the finishing touches on it, all right," muttered Myrtle. "She's probably over there carefully undoing everything you've already done. Puddin will have her feet up on the coffee table, a bag of chips making crumbs on your sofa, and be watching a game show." Puddin was Myrtle's housekeeper. She was completely unreliable in every way; from showing up to doing a good job. Her favorite excuse was that "her back was thrown" whenever Myrtle asked her to do any stooping or scrubbing. The only saving grace to Puddin was her husband, Dusty, who was Myrtle's ancient yardman. Dusty was the only yardman in town who would work around Myrtle's gnomes.

Miles said, "She only does those things at your house. Puddin actually works at mine."

Myrtle made a face. She knew this to be true. "I'm not sure what it is about my house or me that makes Puddin so completely impossible. Send her over here after she's finished at your place. I need some work done." She paused. "Puddin has no intention of *staying* at book club, does she?"

"No."

"Thank goodness. I'm so glad she got over her infatuation with it. For a while, I was really worried," said Myrtle. Puddin had read Myrtle's copy of a book and had been a star at the book club meeting as she made astute observations about a variety of things. This was because it was the book Myrtle had taught from for years and had notes written in the margins.

"The thing is," said Miles, "I'm trying to stay away from large groups of people. I don't want to catch anything, you know."

Myrtle sighed. "You know how these ladies are, Miles. If they have the smallest sniffle, they think it's the end of the world. They take to their beds. They get casseroles from their well-meaning friends. They definitely *don't* go to book club and infect everyone. It's simply not how they operate."

Miles said, "But sometimes people are contagious before they show symptoms. I read a lot about it last night."

Myrtle raised her eyebrows. "You had a busy night between setting up for book club and researching illnesses. I've told you about the danger of reading up on medical stuff online. Now you've got the heebie-jeebies. Book club will be fine. Of course, you could always wear one of those flu masks. *That* will keep everyone away from you. In fact, they might run screaming out of your house."

Miles slumped. "I suppose there's nothing else to do but host it."

"You're right. I'll come over and make sure it all runs smoothly. And I'll be sure to bring an appetizer."

Miles raised his hands as if to ward off evil. "No, that's all right. We have all that covered. We end up with way too much food at these things and then it has to be tossed out. It's such a waste."

Myrtle stared at him. "I don't know what you're talking about. Everyone just takes their leftover food home with them and feeds it to their husbands later. I'd feel badly if I don't bring something."

Before Miles could continue arguing, there was a knock on the door behind him. He opened it up to see Puddin there.

"Figured you was here," she said laconically. "Gest wanted to let you know I was done."

Myrtle said, "Excellent! While you're here, I have some things that I need you to do."

Puddin scowled at her. "Don't got no time for that! Got other things to git to."

Myrtle walked to the door and peered down the street. "Where's your car?"

Puddin muttered, "Done broke again. Dusty'll pick me up."

"Well, Dusty isn't here right now. You can work here until he turns up. You owe me that at the very least, Puddin. It's been ages since you were here. I'm being bullied by gigantic dust bunnies," said Myrtle.

"I'll leave you to it," said Miles quickly. "See you for book club?"

"Of course. You know I wouldn't miss it," said Myrtle. And then promptly forgot about it again as Puddin shambled towards Myrtle's kitchen.

Puddin muttered an imprecation and then her pale, dour face glared around the corner of the kitchen door. "Did you go crazy in here? What's all this stuff?"

"Oh, the stupid junk drawer. I was reorganizing in there and was interrupted," said Myrtle.

"This is organized?" Puddin made a face.

"Look, don't get started with the kitchen. Vacuum the rest of the house first and I'll put that junk away," said Myrtle.

When she looked at everything strewn all over the counter, Myrtle made a face, too. Then she made a command decision and swept it all into the trashcan. If she hadn't needed that stuff in months, she likely wouldn't need it in the future.

The vacuum cleaner turned on and Myrtle kept an eye on Puddin, who was unenthusiastically pushing it around.

"Get under the furniture!" bellowed Myrtle.

Puddin put a hand up to her ear.

"UNDER! Get UNDER!" yelled Myrtle, pointing to the dust bunnies lurking malevolently under her furniture.

Puddin put a hand on her back to indicate that it was thrown.

Myrtle stoically pointed under the furniture until Puddin reluctantly stooped and used the vacuum hose to get the errant bunnies that appeared to be fleeing from the hose.

Dusty did not show up, nor call. Puddin became more and more animated, muttering under her breath at Dusty's tardiness and abject failure in rescuing her.

"Got stuff to *do*," she said, kicking her foot against the door-jamb.

Myrtle was delighted that Dusty had been so unreliable. Puddin had vacuumed, mopped the kitchen, and cleaned her bathtub.

"Do you *really* have something to do, or are you just using that as an excuse?" asked Myrtle.

Puddin said, "I really have stuff to do."

"Stuff like watching your favorite game show? Or real stuff?" asked Myrtle.

Puddin heaved a long-suffering sigh and looked up at Myrtle's ceiling as if looking for divine help in being delivered from annoying elderly women. "Real stuff. I've got to pick up a prescription."

Myrtle raised her eyebrows. "But the pharmacy is open for hours to come. That's hardly an emergency."

Puddin glared at her. "I want to start takin' the medicine now."

"Patience is a virtue," said Myrtle in the tone of someone who actually possessed it.

Puddin set her chin stubbornly.

Myrtle said, "I know what we'll do. I'll drive you there."

Now Puddin squinted up her small eyes. "You?"

"I drive extremely well. And, as it happens, I have an errand to run, myself. I need to go by the used car dealership and trade in the red car for another vehicle," said Myrtle. "You can come along with me and then I'll drive you to the pharmacy and back home."

Puddin considered this while looking suspiciously at Myrtle. "You drive okay?"

"*Extremely well*," repeated Myrtle, looking cross. "Really, I don't know what's wrong with people. Is everyone in this town going deaf but me?"

Puddin said ungraciously, "Guess I'll go with you. Lemme leave Dusty a message."

"While you're leaving him a message, ask him to put my gnomes out in my yard again. I have a bone to pick with Red."

A few minutes later, they were driving toward the dealership.

Puddin was holding onto the passenger door as if her life depended on it.

"That's very distracting," said Myrtle, sounding annoyed.

"Feels right," said Puddin fervently. "Hey, there's a cat over there!"

Myrtle hit the brakes hard enough that their heads bobbed forward.

"The cat was in its yard! Nowhere near the car, Puddin!" scolded Myrtle.

Puddin said sullenly, "Cat could have run into the street. You know what cats is like."

Myrtle made a disgusted noise and accelerated again. Puddin made the sign of the cross.

"And you're Baptist, not Catholic," said Myrtle grouchily.

The dealership was very quiet, which suited Myrtle perfectly. As she drove up, she saw Boone wave away one of his salesmen and come up, smiling, to Myrtle's car.

"Miss Myrtle! You sure do look snazzy behind the wheel of this car." Boone beamed at her, showing way too many teeth. "And this is?" He looked at Puddin, tilting his head to one side as if trying and failing to place her.

"Puddin," said Puddin. She gave a giggle as she was wont to do around attractive men.

Myrtle gave her a repressive look. "Yes, Puddin helps me around the house."

Boone raised his eyebrows. "Does she? I'll have to get your number, Puddin. I know my dad will need some light cleaning now that my poor mom is gone."

Myrtle pursed her lips. She would have to disabuse Boone of the notion that Puddin would actually be anything but trouble. But, she supposed, not in front of Puddin. Otherwise, Puddin might punish her later by refusing to come clean. Then where would she be?

"So, did you like the car?" asked Boone, turning his attention back to Myrtle. "Drives like a dream, doesn't she?"

Myrtle nodded. "It's a very nice car. And I don't want to use up your time too badly, Boone. You don't mind if I drive another car, just to see? Maybe that small black one over there?"

Boone grinned at her. "I like a woman who knows her own mind. No, of course I don't care if you take another one home and see what you think. I want you to find the best car for *you*." He turned the brightness of his smile to Puddin, who simpered. "I don't suppose that you're in the market for a car?"

Puddin stammered out, "Maybe. Depends on the price. My car done broke."

"Past the point of being able to be fixed?" asked Boone in the kind of tone that encouraged a yes answer.

Puddin gave a small shrug, eyes shining at him. "Dunno. My husband ain't figured it out yet."

Boone said sympathetically, "It's hard to find the time, isn't it? And those older cars—I'm guessing yours is older?"

Puddin bobbed her head a few times in eager response.

"When these older cars act out, it's real expensive to make them work again. Sometimes it's cheaper to get a gently used car and not worry about fixing something that's just going to break down again and again," suggested Boone.

Puddin said in a gasping voice, "Maybe I'll come back here later. With Dusty."

Boone grinned at her again, displaying all of his white, sparkling teeth. "Sounds like a plan."

Myrtle said quickly, "By the way, Boone, I'm so sorry to have to extend my condolences again to you. Nell was a special lady."

Boone immediately changed into a more solemn visage. "Yes, she was. And thank you. What a weird morning! Red contacted me right away and was very decent when he let me know. My poor aunt. I don't know what's going on in this town right now. I'm sure Red will get to the bottom of it, though." He paused. "I wish I'd been around whenever that killer dropped by. I'd have taken care of him. But I was at home with my wife, Erin."

Myrtle said, "It was a frightful thing to happen. I simply can't imagine who'd ever want to hurt Nell. Like your mother, she was a real pillar of the community. And her bellringing was delightful."

Boone nodded and heaved a wistful sigh. "If only I could see her again and tell her how much I appreciated her. But that's the thing about life, isn't it? We think we have all the time in the world to share with the people we care about. And no, I can't imagine who could have hurt Aunt Nell."

Myrtle decided she needed to try to open the door to other sides of Nell. Otherwise, they would end up with Saint Nell syndrome. "Of course, she wasn't *perfect*. But even her less-than-perfect traits were lovable."

Boone grinned again. "You mean the way she was bossy? She and Mama used to butt heads all the time over stuff. Nell would try to tell Mama what to do and Mama wouldn't listen to her. Used to drive Nell crazy. In a lot of ways, the two of them were very different, but in other ways, they were a lot alike."

"Sisters," said Puddin in a knowing voice, trying to break into the conversation.

Myrtle pressed her lips together. As if Puddin would know anything about sisters. Now, *cousins* she would know about. She quickly interjected, "How were they alike?"

"You know—they were both really strong, opinionated, organized women. I never went into either Mama's or Nell's house and saw a bunch of clutter or mess of any kind," said Boone. He snorted. "Unless Daddy had made a mess while Mama was out of the house."

Puddin muttered, mostly to herself, "Dusty makes a lot of clutter and mess."

"Daddy is a total slob. But you'd never have known it because Mama would just pick right up after him. He'd lay down a container of yogurt and a spoon and Mama would whoosh in and pick it up, tossing the carton and putting the spoon in the dishwasher. That's how everything stayed immaculate."

"Pearl always did have a lot of energy," said Myrtle.

Boone gave Puddin a smile, "But with Mama gone now and Daddy not exactly at the age to pick up new and better habits, it might be a real good idea for Puddin to start helping out at their house. He's going to have a mountain of trash in there in no time."

Puddin, who'd been smiling fatuously at Boone, suddenly looked crestfallen and then a bit sullen. Myrtle was familiar with this expression of Puddin's. It transpired whenever she realized she might have some work ahead of her.

Boone said, "As for Nell, I'm guessing that it was a burglary gone wrong. Maybe the guy thought that the house was empty, but she was there. When Nell surprised the burglar, he reacted out of fear."

Myrtle said delicately, "Going back to Pearl. You know how things are in a small town, Boone. People talk. Was everything all right between you and your mom?"

Boone's eyebrows now shot up so high that they were lost in the hair that flopped down on his forehead. "You mean somebody said that Mama and I had argued and that maybe I shoved her down the stairs because of it? That's ridiculous!"

"What was the argument about?" asked Myrtle. She wondered if Boone would reference the same argument that Nell had mentioned—that Boone hadn't wanted Pearl to continue driving. Or maybe, there was another argument that he would bring up. Or many others.

Boone frowned. "It wasn't like I fought with Mama all the time. She and I got along real good. But lately, I'd been worried about her safety. She was starting to have little fender-benders in the car. She'd also have a real tough time parking and kept dinging up her car. Mama was getting older and her reflexes weren't so hot." He paused for a second and gave Myrtle his trademark gleaming smile. "No disrespect intended, Miss Myrtle. I know your driving is just fine."

Puddin made a face at this.

"That's all that was about. Me looking out for my Mama. I hate to hear that folks are saying otherwise. They should be very careful about what they say. Considering my position in this town, I would surely sue for slander if I needed to," said Boone.

There was something in his tone that made Myrtle shiver.

He quickly turned back into the over-friendly car salesman. "So, make sure to come back here with your husband, Puddin. I look forward to getting to know y'all and showing you your next car."

Puddin simpered.

Chapter Thirteen

Myrtle was still annoyed as she drove to Puddin's pharmacy. Puddin, on the other hand, was humming to herself.

"Stop that humming, Puddin. It's so off-key that I can't even place the song. Completely irritating."

Puddin, still clutching the passenger side door with one hand, glared at her. "It's obviously 'The Darin' Young Man on the Flyin' Trapeze.'"

"No, it's obviously horrible and needs to stop," said Myrtle shortly. Then she gave Puddin a side glance. "And don't chew your nails."

Puddin set her chin stubbornly and then clung with both hands to the door as they approached the square downtown.

"There's Red again. It seems like all he does is eat," muttered Myrtle as her son wandered out of the police station with a large submarine sandwich in his hand. She gave a jaunty toot of her horn and he turned red in the face at the sight of his mother in a black vehicle with a terrified Puddin in tow.

She navigated the pharmacy drive-through and Puddin got her medicine. Then she set off for Puddin's house to drop her off.

Puddin said, "Maybe Dusty'll have time to go see that car Boone done showed me. What time does they close out there?"

"Late. Probably nine o'clock since people will sometimes go there after work," said Myrtle indifferently.

Puddin sniffed. "Won't clean his daddy's house, though. Filthy."

"Well, I don't know if it's *filthy* yet, but it's likely in a state a lot messier than ninety percent of the houses that you deal with on a regular basis," said Myrtle with a sigh.

Puddin said, "His mama was nice to me, though. An' she was writin' a book."

Now Myrtle turned all her attention on Puddin. This made Puddin screech and point out the windshield. "Th' *road*! There's a kid!"

Myrtle slammed on the brakes. But once again, the reported road hazard was nowhere near the actual road. "Puddin! The child is playing on the playground."

Puddin said sulkily, "Don't mean he won't run into the street."

Myrtle took a deep breath and tried very hard to collect the shreds of her patience. "What do you know about Pearl's book?"

Puddin got a sassy and smug look on her face. She liked being the one who knew things. She especially liked holding such information over people who *didn't* know things. "Jest that she was writin' it. She saw me at the library and we started talkin' about books."

Puddin had recently become more of a reader and would check out books from the library on a monthly basis. She'd gotten her back up when Myrtle had made an assumption about her reading habits (or lack of them.)

Myrtle drove slowly again. "Did she tell you any details about her book?"

"Her was readin' *Grapes of Wrath*," reported Puddin.

"No, the book she was *writing*!" Myrtle's head throbbed.

"Oh, that." Puddin squinted her face up in her typical 'thinking' posture. She was clearly desperate to remember the information and impress Myrtle with her knowledge. "Said it was about secrets."

"What secrets?"

Puddin said, "Somethin' to do about ancient history. Least, that's what she said. Long ago stuff."

"Stuff that might have happened when Boone was a young man?" asked Myrtle sharply.

Puddin obviously badly wanted to be able to offer this information, but it just wasn't there. "Maybe," she said cautiously.

Myrtle said, "I don't know what else it *could* be. History from long ago? Nothing interesting really happened to that family unless she could write about Tara Blanton going missing."

Puddin shrugged. "Don't know nuthin' about that. All she said was that maybe it would give her little girl peace."

"Well, that's an extraordinary thing to have said. And she didn't say anything else? And you didn't ask anything?"

Puddin shrugged again. "She had to go. Somebody came up and started talkin' to her."

Myrtle dropped Puddin off at home and then drove back to her house in something of a fog. She was mulling over all that she'd learned. When she got back home, she noticed a lot of cars on her street and frowned. Then she gasped. "Book club!"

Myrtle hurried inside, cane thumping as she went, and flung open her fridge. Miles had been so insistent that she not bring any food over. His insistence alone was irritating. Under scrutiny, however, the food that she had in her house was rather lacking, at least in terms of its ability to double as an hors d'oeuvres. There was one bunch of lackluster grapes. Its best days were behind it, but that seemed to be the only option. She rinsed them quickly in the sink and then flung them on a plate.

Then she looked at her own reflection. She made a face. Whereas she looked perfectly fine for investigating a murder and going to a car dealership, she didn't really pass for book club. But she was out of time. Myrtle put a little color on her face and then hurried out the door. It was a pity that she didn't have the book. But the fact of the matter is, that book club had fallen off her radar this time. This annoyed her since she was very sensitive to the rare times that she actually forgot things.

Book club was in full swing when she arrived. Miles gave Myrtle a quizzical look when she came in since Myrtle was never late.

"Have a doctor appointment that ran over?" asked Georgia Simpson in a booming voice. Georgia was a tattooed, heavily made-up woman with big hair of various colors. She always had an odd effect on Miles, who appeared to have a strange crush on her. Georgia gave a tremendous laugh which ricocheted through the room.

Myrtle frowned at her. "Why would you imagine I was at the doctors?"

Georgia put out a large hand and clumsily patted Myrtle's sleeve. "Don't be sensitive. Red mentioned the last time I saw him that you've been doing poorly. Besides, it seemed like the obvious choice because you're *never* late. Figured you'd been held hostage at a doctor's office or some other place where you couldn't get freed up." She turned around to a table behind her and turned back around with a large bottle of scotch. "Here, have a drink."

Myrtle gaped at the bottle and then took a few steps up to the table to see it in its entirety. There was a well-represented bar with vodka, gin, scotch, bourbon, and various mixers. She turned to look at Miles, who was miserably stuck in a conversation with Erma Sherman. He gave her a helpless shrug.

Georgia gave her big laugh again. "Have I scandalized you, Miss Myrtle? Sorry. But when the cat's away, the mice will play."

"The cat being Tippy?" asked Myrtle.

Georgia said, "Exactly. Tippy never wants to have drinks at book club because she supposes it would mess up our book discussion time."

Myrtle thought that the book discussion time was pretty messed up already.

"So when I realized that Miles was hosting today and that Tippy wouldn't be here, I thought I'd liven things up. I called up Blanche, who's pretty fun-loving," said Georgia.

Blanche was walking by them at the time and gave Myrtle a saucy wink.

"And you probably wouldn't guess it, but Erma has quite a bar at her house, too. I gave her a little call and she brought in some booze as well. So now we have happy hour," said Georgia.

"And you can walk home, so you can drink just as much as you like."

Suddenly Myrtle, who only drank sparingly and usually sherry at that, felt a bit like a strong drink. It had been a long day and one with many surprises. She had spent a lot of time recently in the company of a used car salesman who may or may not be a murderer. Her son was being exceptionally pushy and was spreading dire rumors about her health. And she hadn't been remotely ready for book club today and wouldn't even be able to make her usual snarky comments about the book. She pressed her lips together and then said, "Make me a bourbon, Georgia. I rarely mix my own drinks. It won't hurt to have the one drink."

Georgia whooped and turned to the bar. What Myrtle didn't know was that Georgia's idea of a normal drink was rather skewed. Georgia fixed it and shoved it at Myrtle, who took a cautious sip of it and made a face.

Georgia howled with laughter. "That expression of yours! That means it's a good drink!"

Myrtle decided that she would hand off the drink to Miles at the first available opportunity. The doorbell rang and Georgia held up a finger. "One second, Miss M. This'll be the pizza." A cheer went up from the assembled women as the door opened to reveal the pizza man.

Myrtle couldn't decide if she'd walked into her usually staid book club or accidentally wandered into a fraternity party.

The pizza delivery man walked in with a stack of pizzas. In return, Georgia gave him a stack of bills. Miles hurriedly directed him to his small kitchen to lay down the pizzas. Georgia said to Myrtle, "Everybody who wanted pizza contributed. Did you want some?"

Myrtle shook her head. "I'd rather have some of Miles's hors d'oeuvres." That was, perhaps, a lie, but not a big one. Miles was looking very gloomy about the alcohol, the pizza, and most likely the assortment of germs wafting around his small home. It might help if she displayed interest in the food he'd prepared. She carefully prepared herself a plate of mini quiches, brie and crackers, and mixed fruit and ignored the cheese pizza that was calling out to her.

Miles sidled up to her a minute later. "Bedlam," he said in a dejected voice.

"On the plus side, Miles, it will go down as a book club meeting to remember," said Myrtle.

"Tippy will hear about it and blame me."

Myrtle said, "Why would she do that? You don't seem to have anything whatsoever to do with this debacle."

"Because I'm the only man. As the only man present, it's my *job* to be blamed," said Miles.

He really seemed to be getting himself into a funk. Myrtle picked up her Georgia-prepared beverage and thrust it at Miles. "Here. You should drink this."

Miles looked at the red plastic cup with misgivings.

Myrtle rolled her eyes. "I took only one sip and I'm perfectly healthy. Besides, the alcohol in this thing would kill any germs intrepid enough to be in the cup."

He took an experimental sip and his eyes opened wide.

"Georgia made it for me," said Myrtle. "I have the feeling that the strength of the beverage is usual for her. We might have to serve her water soon."

They both looked over at Georgia, now laughing uproariously at something Erma said.

Miles looked glum. "For sure. Erma is *never* funny."

"In fact, Miles, the entirety of book club is looking rather . . . happy. It may end up that you're hosting a sleepover here for those who can't make it home."

"Then I'll leave them to it, pack a bag, and head to your guest room," said Miles quickly.

The noise level in the living room was growing to epic proportions. "Miles, you need to call the meeting to order or there won't *be* a book club." Myrtle finished off her brie cheese and crackers and winced as someone's laughter approached hyena level.

Miles appeared reluctant to break the party up.

"None of this is even supposed to be happening," reminded Myrtle. "There should be no liquor. There should be no pizza. There should only be literature and discussion. And perhaps a bit of murder investigating at the tail end of the meeting."

Miles slowly walked over near his front door so he was facing the majority of the chairs. He cleared his throat. Nothing happened.

"Everyone?" he said weakly.

Everyone continued partying.

Myrtle shook her head at him. "Where's your *bell*?" she hollered across the room at him.

Miles shook his head, not able to hear her over the ruckus.

"The *bell*!"

Miles had an antique dinner bell with a long, decorative handle, one of a few nice pieces in his home. Myrtle impatiently glanced around the room for it and spotted it near his silver service on the sideboard. She grabbed it and swung it violently back and forth.

She had to admit that, antique or not, the bell had a nice, rich gong to it. Finally, they had the attention of the room.

Myrtle gave them all a repressive look and drew herself up to her full six feet, looking down at them all. She didn't seem a bit retired in that moment. She seemed as if she hadn't been on any hiatus at all from the classroom. She gazed at her unruly students.

"Thank you!" she said. "Now, it's fine to have fun, but things are getting out of hand."

Most of the book club members looked chastened and contrite. Georgia took another sip from her red plastic cup and gave her a wink.

"Miles has gone to lots of trouble to host us today, so let's give him a thank you," she continued.

Myrtle paused while a bunch of appreciation washed Miles's way. He gave a bob of his head in uncomfortable acknowledgment. Then he took a long drink from his own red plastic cup.

"The first part of our meeting is done and now we'll move on to the book discussion," she said firmly.

The ladies all put down their cups and pizza and obediently took out their books. She turned to Miles and said, "All right, you can lead the discussion."

Miles cleared his throat and walked over to where Myrtle had been. Myrtle sat down. She frowned. It seemed as if the one drink, at least she presumed the one drink, that Miles had enjoyed, had affected him quite a bit.

Miles said, slurring his words, "So, the name of the book is *It's a Ways Out*."

Erma gave her heehawing laugh and called out, "The *title* of the book is *It's a Long Time Coming*."

"Right. What I said," said Miles. He gave a small hiccup. Myrtle narrowed her eyes.

Miles paused and then gazed out the window as if he'd rather be outside. Anywhere but in this room, in fact. He seemed to be grasping for any sort of memory at all about the book. Finally, he said, "In the book, stuff happens."

The book club members gaped at him. This was Miles, after all. Miles who had tried to foist *The Brothers Karamazov* on them in a previous meeting. Who always found some depth in even the shallowest beach reads they'd picked.

"Some of it is bad stuff," he warbled tipsily. "Some of it is good stuff."

Erma appeared to be mightily amused by Miles's impressions of *It's a Long Time Coming*. "What bad stuff?" she asked.

He turned unsteadily to look at Erma. Myrtle stood up again and walked briskly over to Miles. "You don't have to answer that, Miles. You're the host, so why don't you tell everyone to take turns sharing their thoughts on the book? That's what we usually do, after all."

Erma was clearly disappointed at being deprived of her entertainment. "But what did *Miles* think about the story?"

Miles, in the process of being led to an available chair by Myrtle, paused for a second and said, "Bad. It was a bad book."

There was trilling laughter at Miles's newfound lack of fluency as he plopped down into a chair near Myrtle. Myrtle, who wasn't interested in hearing all the assorted impressions of a bad book, leaned in closer to him. "Did you only drink that one drink?"

Miles gave another small hiccup and gave Myrtle a sorrowful look. "Just the one you gave me."

Myrtle sighed. "Either you're a real lightweight or else Georgia makes a really stiff drink. Just stay put and out of trouble until this meeting is over with."

Which, by the look of things, would take a while. It seemed to take forever for the tipsy book club members to collect their thoughts. When they finally did, their thoughts were not worth sharing. They rambled through their impressions of the book with no coherency at all until their little speeches shambled to a stop.

Book club member Blanche at least seemed to realize her own limitations. She held up the book and said with a shrug, "I can't discuss it, but it was a pretty good read."

Myrtle appreciated her honesty and brevity. So much so, in fact, that when it came to be her own time, she said, "I'll admit that I didn't read this book. I've been very busy lately and it sort of slipped my mind. That being said, it sounds like a decent story. However, there are so many *stellar* reads out there that I don't see myself putting it on my to-be-read list."

There was a handful of applause after Myrtle spoke and a couple of the women looked admiringly at her for having gone to book club and not even opened the cover of the book being discussed.

Miles leaned in. "Good point."

Myrtle shrugged. "Well, if I haven't read *Ulysses* or *The Sound and the Fury*, I'm certainly not going to waste whatever time I have left on the pablum being peddled at this meeting."

Miles nodded. His eyes were half-closed.

"For heaven's sake, Miles! Pull yourself together," snapped Myrtle. "You're passing out at book club."

The words, so incongruous, made Miles recover somewhat. He sat up straight in his seat and blinked a few times.

"Do you want me to close the meeting?" asked Myrtle in her stage whisper. There were only two women left to discuss the book.

Miles nodded. "Might be best. We're a team effort."

She understood what he was saying although the words were slurred. So after the discussion was through, she stood up to take care of the small bit of business that the book club meetings covered. "Thank you all for coming and for lending your thoughts on this month's selection. Since Miles hosted, it's his turn to select a book."

Miles glanced around the room. Erma was ignoring the business part of the meeting altogether and was having a very lively conversation with Georgia, who was hooting her laughter loudly, in response. Blanche, her own part of discussing the book now over, was pouring what looked like a stiff drink. Libby Holloway had attempted to make herself a plate of pizza, but had dropped it on the floor and was red-faced and making another.

"I pick *Lord of the Flies*," drawled Miles.

Myrtle's eyes twinkled. "*Lord of the Flies*, it is! An interesting tale of what happens when a group of civilized people end up going wild. And please—everyone take care on the way home. Many of you are in walking distance: and there's nothing wrong with a little exercise."

Unfortunately, most of the book club members did not seem to get the cue that the meeting was now over. They all returned to the bar and refilled their drinks, laughing uproariously and now talking very loudly. Miles was holding his head as if it hurt from the noise.

The door opened and Myrtle raised her eyebrows in surprise. Whoever was late to this book club meeting was *very* late. The members should be on their way to their cars. She raised her eyebrows even higher when she saw Elaine walk through the door with Jack in tow. Elaine looked around her in bemusement at the ordinarily decorous book club which now resembled a bacchanal. She had, Myrtle noted with amusement, a camera around her neck.

Chapter Fourteen

When Elaine spotted Myrtle, she carefully led Jack over toward her. This was difficult because of the chairs in the way, and also because Margaret Goodner was swaying on her feet between them.

When she finally reached Myrtle, Myrtle shook her head. "Sorry that you had to see this debauchery, Elaine. And poor Jack."

Jack, however, seemed focused solely on the pizza. There were still several boxes of it and he was eyeing it hungrily.

"No, this is *wonderful*!" said Elaine. "I needed another photo for Sloan for the paper. He promised me I could put something else in as filler. I mean, I *like* putting photos up on the paper's social media, but it seems much more authentic to have it in print. I thought everyone would be all stiff and polite and not want their pictures taken. But they're so relaxed. This is *perfect*."

Myrtle looked doubtfully at the room. "Not my definition of perfect, but go right ahead. They certainly are *relaxed*."

And very happy. There was still a lot of raucous laughter. Unwisely, no one seemed to be alarmed or on alert about the fact that someone was taking pictures. Including Miles, who appeared to be taking a short nap.

Georgia sidled up to Myrtle again. "Good meeting!" she bellowed. "Tippy should go out of town more often."

Tippy would be horrified when she returned from her trip and saw the pictures in the paper of her book club. Myrtle was ready to talk of other things.

"I suppose so," she said. "Listen, Georgia, I have a question for you. I can't totally remember when you went to school, although I know I taught you. Are you roughly the same age as Pearl Epps's kids?"

Georgia's face grew solemn. "Older. But my younger sister, Peggy, was their age. Such a mess about Pearl, isn't it? What's Red think about all of it?"

Myrtle made a face. "As if Red would share what he thinks with me. You know him better than that. He's just trying to pick through the evidence and talk to people and figure out what happened to Pearl and Nell."

Georgia shook her head. "Sure seems crazy. Peggy was pretty good friends with Rose back in the day. Course, she don't live here anymore." She saw the look on Myrtle's face and hastily corrected herself. "*Doesn't* live here anymore. Sorry. It's the booze talking."

"Do you remember much about the time surrounding when Tara Blanton went missing?" asked Myrtle.

Georgia said, "A little. Peggy talked a good deal about it at the time. She was real upset. Tara was a friend of hers, too, because Rose hung out with her all the time. And Boone was dating Tara."

Myrtle raised her eyebrows. "Boone was *dating* her? But I'd never heard anything about that."

"Tara's parents weren't real happy about their daughter dating Boone," said Georgia. "But Boone talked about it all the time at school."

Myrtle frowned. It had been a long time. "I know he was very mischievous in class. Spitballs and passing notes and whatnot. Actually, he's sort of mischievous even now. But I didn't realize that he was all that bad that parents wouldn't like him."

Georgia said, "Well, sometimes people act out at home where they don't at school. Yeah, Boone was a kind of bad boy. He drank a lot, smoked, did all that kind of stuff. Was sort of disrespectful, too. I remember one day that Peggy was hanging out with Rose and Boone and invited them to come over to our house. Daddy wouldn't let Boone in the door."

Myrtle said with a chuckle, "That must have been awkward."

"Oh, Peggy was very tearful over it, but Daddy was determined. Boone ended up leaving and Rose stayed for a while, but it was definitely weird after that."

Myrtle nodded. "So Tara wisely kept quiet about the fact that she and Boone were dating."

"A secret from Mom and Dad," said Georgia, bobbing her head. "Because Tara was a good girl and wasn't the sort to get into any trouble. And she didn't *want* any trouble, either. Boone was pretty charismatic and was a big deal at the high school. They just kept their relationship on the down-low."

Myrtle said slowly, "But that would have been important for the police to know. Boone should probably have been considered a suspect."

Georgia shrugged. "Suspect in what? As far as the police were concerned, Tara Blanton ran away. That's what they wanted to think, anyway. Sure made life easier for them that way. If there weren't no crime . . . uh, *wasn't* a crime, then you didn't have to worry about suspects, did you?"

Myrtle said, "But there was talk at the time that Tara had *mentioned* running away."

Georgia gave a short laugh. "Talk? From who? Not *Tara*. Somebody said that because they were trying to cover up what really happened."

"What did you and Peggy think when Tara just disappeared like that?"

Georgia said, "That something bad had happened to her. Because Tara had a great life. Her grades were good, her parents loved her, and she had a popular boyfriend. There was absolutely nothing going on in her life that she should have wanted to run away from. Besides, there was that party. Something could have gone wrong during the party."

"What party?" Myrtle leaned in closer.

"Oh, Boone and Rose's folks were going out of town. You know what that means. Everybody knew that there would be a party at their house," said Georgia with a snort.

"I didn't know that," said Myrtle. She scowled. "Did Red go? Did *you* go?"

Georgia gave her guffawing laugh. "Red? Is he really going to get into trouble when that party happened thirty years ago? As a matter of fact, I *did* go to the party, but I left before long. I thought it was kind of lame. And I don't remember Red there at all."

"Why did you think the party was lame?" asked Myrtle.

Georgia yawned, showing off her cavernous mouth and quite a few dental fillings in the process. Whether she was bored with the conversation or finally feeling the effects of the alcohol, Myrtle wasn't sure.

Georgia answered, "I dunno. I didn't like the music they were playing and all the kids there were younger than me and immature. It just wasn't my scene, so I left."

"And Tara was there?" asked Myrtle.

Georgia looked briefly annoyed at repeating herself. "Yep. That's where she was. I'd have told the cops, too, if anybody had cared to question me about it. But nobody did."

"Was she getting along well with everybody there?" asked Myrtle.

Georgia said, "You're talking about something that took place practically a lifetime ago, Miss M. But yeah, I still do remember some details because it all stuck in my head when Tara went missing that night. Tara had been drinking, for one."

"Drinking?" Myrtle looked startled.

Georgia grinned at her. "I'm surprised that you're surprised. You dealt with teenagers all those years. I'd-a guessed that you knew all the ins and outs of teen behavior."

"And I did. But the fact is that Tara didn't seem to be interested in that kind of thing. She seemed, actually, like a really sweet, innocent girl," said Myrtle. "Now I've no doubt that Boone Epps was drinking like crazy."

"You're right there," said Georgia, wagging a finger at her. "He was almost off his head with booze. Wasn't the kind of guy who could hold his liquor."

From what Myrtle had just observed of Georgia, she could likely hold hers better than any man. "Okay," she said, "so Boone and Tara were both drinking. Anything else?"

"Tara and Rose had a spat," said Georgia succinctly. She took another swig from her cup.

"Did they? About what?" asked Myrtle.

Georgia shrugged. "It just didn't seem all that important at the time, Miss M. These were teenagers and teenagers act out sometimes. I only know that they'd had a falling out."

She wagged her finger at Myrtle. "Speaking of falling outs, I saw *another* spat yesterday. Boone was yelling at his sister like you wouldn't believe. She was crying her eyes out and he was really letting her have it."

"When was this? And where?" asked Myrtle.

"On this very same street. Not too far from the Epps house . . . and not too far from Nell's either, I reckon. I guess Rose was dog walking because she had Tippy's two standard poodles with her. And Boone was leaning out of his car window and his face was like thunder."

She looked balefully into her empty plastic cup. "I gotta get this thing filled again," she said as if it were the most onerous task. "See ya soon."

A full forty-five minutes later, the herd of cackling women had finally filed out to walk themselves home or to have their husbands or daughters pick them up.

Miles looked around his once-tidy home with a shocked expression. The state of his house appeared to sober him up. The women had certainly not cleaned up after themselves, which was an anomaly in itself. They'd also left various things behind them by accident—Myrtle spotted at least two sets of car keys, a purse, and numerous copies of *It's a Long Time Coming*.

"What a nightmare," he said. He hesitated. "I believe I might have dropped off back there for a few minutes. Did I miss anything?"

"Only Elaine. She came in and took pictures for the newspaper," said Myrtle.

Miles held his head again.

"I'll have to call Puddin," he muttered, picking up a paper plate with a pizza carcass on it before hastily setting it down again as grease got on his fingers.

"Puddin? You're clearly delusional. Puddin wouldn't have anything to do with a mess this large. No, you need an actual professional cleaning service to come in or else you'll need to spend the next few hours getting everything back to normal," said Myrtle.

Miles put his hands to his head as he walked around to survey the damage. "I wonder if I can get the service that Blanche is using now."

"You can get *anybody* for the right price. Aside from Puddin," amended Myrtle. "There are other housekeepers available. It's just that they cost a fortune."

"I'll call Blanche's housekeeper," he said decisively. "I can't handle the scope of this mess. And then let's go to your house. I don't even want to look at it."

Myrtle's house was startlingly clean in comparison, since Puddin had actually done a little work while she'd been there.

Miles was clutching his head again. "I must have picked up some sort of illness at book club."

"The only illness that you picked up is a hangover. I'll make us some strong coffee," said Myrtle briskly, walking over to her coffeemaker.

Miles said, "But then we won't be able to fall asleep tonight. Book club lasted so late that it's practically time to turn in now."

"When do we ever really fall asleep? No matter what we do, we won't be able to get a good night's sleep, so we might as well enjoy the coffee," said Myrtle.

She bustled around, making the coffee. Miles jumped when there was a scratching sound at the window.

"Darling Pasha!" said Myrtle proudly. "Hungry again." She gasped. "Miles! We forgot about the cat food sale."

Miles, who did not have any desire to discuss cat food or, really, anything else, groaned. "But the sale goes on the entire week. We don't have to go tonight."

"The sale may go on for the entire week, but today is senior citizen's day, so I get an additional discount. What's more, they're running a one-day double-coupon deal," said Myrtle.

Miles buried his face in his hands. "Those coupons are too high to double, Myrtle. They only double the fifty-cent or seventy-five cent ones."

"Usually that's the case. But today it's *super* double coupon day. They double the value up to a dollar."

Miles waved a hand. "I surrender. Let's go to the store. But can we at least drink that coffee first? The store is in no danger of closing at this hour."

Myrtle nodded. She fed Pasha, who ravenously dug in to her food. Then she poured them two cups of coffee, just how they liked them. "The book club meeting was very interesting this afternoon." She put a cup of coffee in front of Miles.

Miles asked, "Was it?" in a very doubtful tone.

"Well, everyone was too intoxicated to ask either of us about poor Nell and poor Pearl. Ordinarily, they'd have been peppering us with questions. That was, perhaps, the only good part about the alcohol at the meeting." Myrtle took a cautious sip of her coffee. Despite all the cream in it, it was still very hot.

"The alcohol was actually very nice for about twenty minutes," said Miles.

Myrtle said, "And then it led to that dreadful book club discussion."

Miles looked morosely into his coffee cup. "It was a dreadful book, so it naturally followed that it would engender a dreadful discussion."

Myrtle pinched her lips together. She refrained from telling Miles that the worst parts were his own startlingly insipid thoughts on the story. He had been most un-Miles-like. Instead she said, "I meant, however, that there were other aspects of the book club meeting that were interesting."

Miles raised his eyebrows. "Did you find out any information about Nell's death?"

"Maybe indirectly," said Myrtle. "It was more about what happened to Tara Blanton."

Miles raised his eyebrows even higher. "Was this information provided by Georgia? I saw how much time you were spending talking to her. An unusual amount of time, I thought, given that it was . . . Georgia."

"She had a good deal to say about Tara because Georgia's younger sister and she were good friends."

Miles drank more of his coffee and now seemed a good deal more animated. That might have to do with the caffeine in the cup. If Georgia had made a stiff drink, Myrtle had made a stiff coffee. "Let me guess. Georgia said that Tara hadn't run away."

"Exactly. She said that the cops were looking for the easiest way out of an investigation. Georgia was adamant that there was no reason for Tara to run away. She said that she had lots of friends, had a great home life, and was doing well at school. What's more, she said that Tara and Boone were secretly dating," said Myrtle.

"Really? And no one told the police that at the time?" asked Miles.

"It sounded as if the police really didn't want to know," said Myrtle with a shrug. "What's more, Boone and Rose were hosting a party the night of Tara's disappearance and Tara was there at the party. Fortunately, Red was not." Myrtle's face was dark.

"Luckily for him, judging from your expression," said Miles. "Can one really get in trouble for a teenage infraction thirty years later?"

"One can suffer by perpetually viewing a large collection of rather darling gnomes across the street," said Myrtle. "Which I need to have Dusty pull out anyway for all the trouble Red is giving me."

Miles said, "So let me get this straight. Tara was secretly dating Boone, for unknown reasons."

"Boone had a reputation for being something of a wild child and Tara's parents wouldn't have permitted it," said Myrtle.

"Then she went to a party that, I'm guessing, resembled our book club meeting," continued Miles.

"Except on a greater scale," said Myrtle. "And one other detail—she argued with Rose at some point during the proceedings."

"Then she disappeared. And everyone decided that she'd run away." Miles paused. "This ineptitude is making my head hurt again."

Myrtle poured more coffee into his mug and shoved the cream and sugar at him.

Fortunately, Miles rallied a bit more at the infusion of caffeine and they set off for the grocery store. Myrtle insisted on driving.

"Remind me why you need me to come along, since you have a vehicle at your disposal?" asked Miles.

"You're here for your muscles, Miles. I can't possibly lug a few cases of cat food out to the car. Not holding my cane."

Miles looked glumly at his arms. "I'm not sure I have the requisite muscles. Isn't there a teenage neighbor who can be bribed to do this sort of errand?"

"But that negates the whole 'saving money' aspect! I'm trying to spend as little as possible on this purchase," said Myrtle. "And I'm sure your muscles are up to the task."

They walked into the small store, which was locally owned and in competition with the Piggly-Wiggly. Myrtle had little loyalty to either and was there to shop deals. "Is there anything else that we need?" she asked, frowning at the aisles.

Miles said, "I should probably point out that there has been another death. Is another casserole—cassoulet—required? Because it would be better if we just picked something up here. They have a decent deli section."

"It might be a good way to visit Rose," mused Myrtle. "After all, it's hard to catch her between all of her random jobs." She looked over the deli offerings and made a face. "It's all rather pedestrian, isn't it? The offerings aren't exactly haute cuisine."

Miles's face was grave. "Myrtle, this is good, plain food. I'm sure that Rose, living alone, isn't used to anything more sophisticated than this. It's no fun to cook for one, as we both know."

Myrtle sighed. "I suppose you're right. So which will it be: chicken and penne pasta, or meatloaf with a side of potatoes?"

"I vote for the meatloaf," said Miles.

"And since your opinion is unerringly male, I'll get the chicken pasta," said Myrtle decisively. She plopped the container in her cart. "I guess I'll put it in one of my own casserole dishes later." She squinted across the grocery store and grabbed Miles's arm. "Isn't that Edward over there? In the canned meats?"

Chapter Fifteen

Miles peered over and nodded. "It is. I suppose no one has been giving him casseroles, since his relationship with Nell wasn't public."

Myrtle said, "We can talk to him on the way over to the cat food aisle."

Miles balked. "Approaching him in the grocery store? He's just lost someone really close to him. He might not feel much like talking."

"All the better to offer our condolences." Myrtle walked toward the canned meats with great determination. Miles gave a small sigh and hurried to keep up, pushing the cart as he followed.

Myrtle said, "Edward?"

Edward turned around sharply, apparently deep in his thoughts. He slumped a little when he saw Myrtle. "Hello there," he said in a resigned voice.

"I'm so sorry about Nell. She was a wonderful lady," said Myrtle.

Miles said, "Sorry about this." He might have been speaking about Nell or about the fact that they were pestering Edward in a grocery store.

Edward said, "No, it's all right. Actually, I'm glad I ran into you. I heard you were the ones who found her, right? The police wouldn't give me any information, and I was hoping that you could."

Myrtle and Miles exchanged a look. Myrtle said, "She didn't suffer at all." She crossed her fingers because she doubted that was actually the case. "And she obviously let whoever it was in. It must have been someone she knew because the door was open. That's how Miles and I went in. We're just very sorry." Myrtle hoped that this small amount of information was enough for Edward to stop asking questions. Although it certainly wasn't much.

Edward, though, took Myrtle's assurances that Nell hadn't suffered like a man being offered a lifeboat. Relief spread over his features. "That's good to hear, Myrtle. Thanks. I'm just devastated over this. I've been very busy lately, and I hadn't seen Nell for the last couple of days." His eyes clouded over and got a bit misty. He blinked them furiously, and the mist dissipated.

Myrtle was relieved. The last thing she wanted to do was to try to bolster up an emotional old man. She said, "You've been busy?"

Miles gave her a repressive look. Her tone reflected her incredulity instead of coming across as a straight question.

Edward heard it too. "Yes. Now, I've taken *breaks* from my busyness. You've seen me on breaks."

Miles hopped in. "I suppose Nell likely wanted some space after her sister's unexpected death?"

Edward gave him a grateful look. "Yes. That's it. That's it, exactly. You know how some people are—they want to lick their wounds in private. Naturally, I saw Nell right after I got word about what happened to Pearl, but after that, I gave her some space to try and absorb what had happened."

Myrtle said, "Did you talk with her on the phone at all?"

Edward shook his head. "No. I'd told her that I'd see her at Pearl's funeral. That's the last I heard from her. I was waiting for the funeral before I saw her again. Then there'd be a little closure, and I figured maybe she'd be ready to spend some time with other people."

"As it happens, I've been looking for a new car. Well, a new *used* car," said Myrtle. "I've spoken with Boone."

Edward's face reddened. Myrtle gave him a wary look. The *other* thing she didn't need was to have an old guy have a heart attack right in front of her.

He said in a combative tone, "What did Boone have to say about all this? About Nell?"

Miles stepped in again since he seemed to have a calming effect on Edward. "He didn't say anything bad at all. He thought maybe it was a burglary gone wrong. He couldn't imagine who could possibly have wanted to murder Nell."

Edward said gruffly, "Exactly. It must have been somebody in that nutty family."

Myrtle raised her eyebrows. "You think so? You seem surer of that than you were the first time we talked after Pearl's death."

"Who else would it be?" Edward shrugged. "And Boone's explanation is patently ridiculous. He just doesn't want any suspicion to fall on him or his family. Of *course,* it has to be someone in the family, as crazy as that sounds." Edward leaned on his shopping cart, staring at the canned contents as if they held the answer. "It must be Rose. She's kooky enough to have done it."

Miles said, "You believe that she pushed her mother down the stairs and then *murdered* her aunt?"

Edward winced at the mention of Nell's murder. "Why not? As frail as she seems, she's surprisingly strong. The girl walks all day long. And she has quite a temper on her. There's no reason at all why she shouldn't have been *able* to do it. She's quite a bit stronger than both Pearl and Nell would have been. What's more, she's been spending a *lot* of time with Nell lately."

Myrtle said, "You mean in the last couple of days? When you've been so busy?"

A slight smile played on Miles's lips.

Edward gave her a sharp look. "Yes, in the last couple of days. As a matter of fact, I frequently drive past Nell's house on the way to errands and whatnot. I've seen Rose's car there."

Myrtle said, "Well, surely that's to be expected. Her mother is recently deceased. Maybe she was looking to Nell to be a sort of mother figure to her. Or maybe Nell reminded her of Pearl and it comforted her to spend time with her."

Edward made a face, "It's not like Pearl and Nell were *that* much alike."

Miles said, "But you believe that Rose might not have been over there with the best intentions? That she could be dangerous?"

"I certainly think it's possible. She's quite mercurial in mood. You'd know if you spent any time with her," said Edward.

Myrtle remembered the scene at the Goodwill when Rose yelled at her father for giving away her mother's things.

"Now, it was good to see you, but I must finish my shopping trip," said Edward severely. "I have ice cream at the bottom of my cart and it's going to melt everywhere if this continues. Have a good day."

Miles and Myrtle loaded the cat food into Myrtle's car. Or, rather, Miles did and Myrtle supervised.

"We're heading back home?" asked Miles hopefully.

"Let's not. We headed back home yesterday and look what happened."

"I hardly think Nell's death was our fault," said Miles.

"If we'd figured out who was responsible for Pearl's death, Nell's death would never have happened." Myrtle waved her hands in the air, a gesture that made Miles clutch the door.

"The car isn't even moving, Miles!" said Myrtle.

Miles released the door. "If we're not going back home, then where *are* we going? Because it's been a long day, Myrtle. Book club was crazy. We should persuade Elaine to keep those photos out of the newspaper. Plus the fact that we have groceries in the car."

"The 'groceries' are just cans of cat food. They're not going to spoil in the next hour or so," said Myrtle.

"Plus, I want to make sure that my house is in good shape and secure. I've never used this cleaning service, even if they do come highly recommended. I could arrive and discover that they left my front door wide open and took all my valuables."

Miles appeared to be getting himself more worked up. He took out his hand sanitizer and squirted it on both palms. "Plus, we've been in the grocery store and I'm not even sure how many germs must have been in there. I would like to wash my hands instead of using this alcohol-based stuff that dries out my skin."

Myrtle opened her mouth to argue, but saw the stubborn set of Miles's chin. She knew when she was beaten. "All right," she said with a sigh. "But if there are any more bodies, that's on you, Miles."

"I'll take full responsibility." Miles rolled his eyes.

Myrtle was still mulling over the case as she backed up out of the parking space. Miles clutched the door again.

"You know, Edward might have been right about Rose and her moods. Perhaps she's not really the best candidate for Sloan," said Myrtle.

"I could have told you that. She has too much going on right now to embark on a relationship," said Miles. "We should butt out of Sloan's business. Clearly, there's not the perfect woman right now for him. Maybe soon there will be."

Myrtle said as she maneuvered the car onto their street, "The thing is, I keep remembering how emotional Rose was when I saw her at the Goodwill. She was *not* ready to part with her mother's things. It was a little weird that messy old Hubert who needs a housekeeper was so eager to get rid of all of his wife's things."

"Well, if you're thinking that the missing laptop could be in that mess, you're wrong. The police went over that house with a fine-toothed comb, I'm sure. Besides, there's a difference between being sloppy with your dishes and clothes and not wanting sad reminders of your recently deceased wife around," said Miles.

"I suppose. But the main point is that Rose was over-wrought. Frail as she seems, she's a strong suspect," said Myrtle.

"What about Edward? If you're looking for people who were recently very emotional, it seems like he fits the bill. We've heard that he was the one who was most violently upset when Pearl announced that her book was finished," said Miles.

Myrtle pulled the car into Miles's driveway. "I can see him giving Pearl a little shove down the stairs. Although I'm not quite sure why Edward would have *been* upstairs alone with Pearl. *That* part I'm not at all sure about."

"Perhaps he had to help her move something heavy. It doesn't have to be some sort of nefarious reason. Maybe her printer didn't work, and he was helping her to fix it. Then he just tipped her right over the stairs," suggested Miles.

"Do we see Edward as the sort who knows how to fix faulty printers? He hangs out with a group of old guys in front of the diner all day," said Myrtle.

Miles shrugged.

Myrtle said, "What's more, do we see Edward murdering *Nell*? And why would he do such a thing? He got all misty-eyed when he was talking about her earlier. From all accounts, he was very protective of her."

"Maybe they had some sort of heated argument and things got out of hand," said Miles.

Myrtle looked at Miles through narrowed eyes. "So Edward's your pick for it. I suspect this has more to do with the fact that you're bitter that you're not part of the group of old guys. You want to be in the in-crowd."

"Are *they* the in-crowd?" Miles looked startled.

Myrtle sighed. "Never mind. All right, we'll keep Edward in as a suspect. Although I do think there are better prospects." She stopped talking and squinted at Miles's front porch. "What's that thing over there?"

"What thing?" Miles leaned forward and peered through the windshield.

"That thing slumped in the chair on your front porch. Did you leave some old clothes out?"

"Of course not! Maybe the housekeeper left a jacket or something. Wait—is that Wanda?" asked Miles.

They quickly hopped out of the car and hurried up toward the front porch to find that the slumped clothing was indeed a napping Wanda, head resting on her curled-up hands on the arm of the wicker chair on Miles's front porch. She startled awake when Myrtle's cane thumped vigorously on the pathway.

Miles stooped in front of her. "Wanda? Are you all right?"

A single tear made its way down her thin cheek. She shook her head.

Chapter Sixteen

A minute later they'd bustled Wanda into Miles's now-gleaming kitchen. Miles made coffee and Myrtle dug up leftovers that she heated and shoved in front of Wanda. Wanda watched them listlessly.

"Got to tell you somethin'," she grated.

"First, you must eat. For heaven's sake, you'd collapsed out there!" said Myrtle.

Wanda shook her head. "Napping."

"Well, it sure didn't look like napping. It looked like 'passed out.' Now go ahead and eat this stuff." Myrtle studied the food. "It looks like roast beef and potatoes and I'm sure it's good if Miles made it. He can only cook four things, but each one of them is like an art form."

Miles put the coffee, black as Wanda preferred it, in front of the woman. They watched as she inhaled the food and drank the hot coffee down, wincing as she did. Finally, she pushed the plate away from her.

"Feel better?" demanded Myrtle in a tone that suggested that the answer really needed to be 'yes.'

Wanda nodded and took a deep, shuddering breath. "She's dead."

"Nell? Yes. I'm sorry, but I'd have thought you'd have known that," said Myrtle with a frown.

Wanda shook her head. "No, the girl."

"Rose?" Miles looked horrified.

Wanda sighed. "No, the *little* girl. That Tara."

"I thought we'd established that earlier," said Myrtle, still frowning. "At least, you'd told me that was the case."

"She's dead an' I know where th' body is," said Wanda with effort. She shivered.

Myrtle's eyes widened. Then she turned on Miles. "Miles! It's freezing cold in here. Wanda is turning blue! Don't you have blankets or heavy coats or gloves or something for her?"

Miles hurried off and returned quickly with some old multicolored afghans that looked like elderly relatives from long ago had made them. He slipped one gently around Wanda's skinny shoulders and then draped another one on her lap that hung to the floor.

Myrtle leaned in and said carefully, "Now, Wanda, is this something new? Because I'm pretty sure I don't remember this level of certainty from you the last time we talked about Tara Blanton."

Wanda gave a weary nod. "Knew she was dead, but didn't know where. Now I do."

Myrtle said, "Well then, we'll have to give Red a phone call."

Miles shifted uncomfortably on his feet. "Are you sure that's the right thing to do?"

Myrtle stared at him. "Of *course,* it's the right thing to do! That's what we *always* do, Miles. When there's a body, we always call Red."

"Not immediately," pointed out Miles.

"Maybe not always in the first five minutes, but *sometimes* in the first five minutes," said Myrtle. "You're acting as if we're heading into new and uncharted territory."

Wanda looked down at the table and then looked back up at Myrtle. "He don't want Red to think I'm crazy."

"Crazy? Why on earth would he think that? You write an incredibly detailed column in the paper every week giving very specific horoscopes to various residents. If that's not proof of your gifts, I don't know what is," said Myrtle.

Wanda gave her a small smile that seemed a bit pitiful. As if maybe she knew what this future conversation with Red would hold.

Miles said, "All I'm saying is that usually there is a body directly in front of us when we make our call to Red. This is more of a *hypothetical* body." He held up his hands as if to ward off an onslaught from Myrtle. "Hypothetical to *Red*, at any rate."

"He'd jump on any credible information that he can at this point. It's very likely tied into his current investigation," said Myrtle with a sniff.

Miles glanced at Wanda's emaciated form, still covered with brightly colored afghans as if he wasn't at all sure how credible her information would appear.

Wanda croaked at Miles. "Sorry 'bout the horoscope."

Miles's eyes widened. "The horoscope? About the germs? The horoscope was . . . incorrect?"

"It was an out-and-out lie," drawled Wanda, looking down at the floor. "But didn't need you to go to the doctor with Myrtle and me. Woulda messed the order of everything up."

Miles and Myrtle exchanged looks as if not at all sure what exactly this meant. Did everything really have a cosmically prescribed order?

Myrtle said, "Well, thank goodness we don't have to worry about Miles getting contaminated any longer. And now I'm calling Red."

Red stared at the scene in front of him. Wanda was still swaddled in blankets and shivering. Miles had pulled out more food, this time of the carbohydrate variety, and lined it up in front of Wanda in a sort of salty buffet. Myrtle had her arms crossed, appeared to be on at least her third cup of coffee, and was staring at him with a ferocious expression.

"What's going on here, y'all?" asked Red in a deliberately patient voice. "Mama, you said you had information about the case." He sat down across from Wanda at the kitchen table, pulled out a small spiral notebook and a stubby pencil, and looked at the assembled group expectantly.

"It ties into the case. There's a small difference," said Myrtle. "Wanda has something to tell you."

Red turned to Wanda and said with a forced smile, "Wanda?"

Wanda took a deep, shuddering breath and looked at Myrtle.

Myrtle said, "Wanda is having a hard evening. The fact of the matter is that Wanda knows where Tara Blanton's body is."

Red dropped the notebook and absently picked it up from his lap. "Tara Blanton. From thirty-odd years ago."

Myrtle gave a stiff nod. "That is correct. One of your class-mates. And I was very glad to hear that you hadn't attended the big party at the Epps house."

Red gave a big sigh as if to try and calm himself down. "I doubt the Epps family has been in a partying mood, Mama."

"The party the children had when you were in *high school*. Pay attention, Red!" scolded Myrtle.

Red turned again to Wanda. He said gently, "So you're say-ing that you have some sort of information about Tara Blanton. That she didn't run away. That she's actually dead. And that you know where her body is located?"

Wanda nodded, looking away from Red. She grated, "In their yard."

"Whose yard?" pressed Red.

"Them kids. Boone and Rose."

Red put his notebook and stubby pencil on the table and rubbed both hands over his face. "And how did you come about this information, Wanda?"

Myrtle snapped, "How do you *think* she did, Red? She has a gift."

Red stared at her and then repeated, "Wanda, how did you come about this information? It's been quite a long time since Tara disappeared. I was in high school and I'm pushing fifty now."

Wanda said with weary resignation, "Had a vision, Red. Sor-ry."

Myrtle stood up impatiently. "What are we doing here at the house still? We should be on the way over to the Epps house."

Red said, "Right. We'll just head over to see grieving Hubert Epps and tell him we're bringing in a team to dig up his yard to look for a girl who disappeared thirty years ago. I'm sure he'll be delighted to hear that."

Wanda shrugged. "It's true."

Red stared at her again for a few moments and then said, "Did you know the Epps family, Wanda? You're roughly my age."

It was hard to nail down Wanda's age, actually. She could either be very old or very young. The only thing that really stood out was the damage that life had inflicted on her.

Wanda gave him a small, sad smile. "You know I didn't go to school, Red. Didn't know them kids."

Myrtle said fiercely, "Why are you wasting our time, Red? Let's bundle Wanda up and take her over to Hubert's house and have her point out where Tara's body is. I won't have you continuing to badger her and make insinuations."

Red sighed again. "I'm not happy about this. I really don't know how I can explain this to Lieutenant Perkins."

Miles said, "Perhaps you could say that an anonymous informant has given you a pertinent tip?"

Red pointed at him. "That might work. Okay, that's what we're going with. But in that case, we don't need to bring Wanda along with us."

"Then how will the police find the body?" demanded Myrtle. "They really *would* have to dig up Hubert's entire lawn."

"The state police have cadaver dogs," said Red.

Miles's eyes widened. "They can even find . . . bones?"

"They sure can. I can't explain it . . . well, any more than I can explain Wanda's weird hunches . . . but that's what they do. Lemme make a phone call."

Red stepped into the back of Miles's house to make the call. When he came back out, he said, "They're going to be here a lot sooner than I thought. They're already a county over responding to a missing person at a state park. I'm going to go over and talk to Hubert. It would be best if he could give permission for us being on his property, otherwise we've got to get a warrant. Hoping he'll just cooperate."

Myrtle stood up and Red shook his head. "Nope. Y'all need to stay here."

"Stay *here*?" Myrtle waved a hand around the room as if to indicate that Miles's small, tidy home was a horrific dungeon.

"That's exactly right. Or stay over at your own house if Miles needs his back. All I need is for Wanda to be out there shivering in the dark and me trying to explain why she's there to a bunch of guys from the state police. No way." Red picked up his keys and headed for the door. "I'll be back later and give you an update." His voice was firm.

Waiting for the update became rather tedious. First, they turned on the television, but the only things on were some sport teams no one knew and game shows with hyperactive hosts. Then they tried to sit and read. Miles was a poetry fan and Myrtle had pulled out his Edna St. Vincent Millay, but Wanda was sitting very listlessly since she wasn't exactly a reader.

Finally, Myrtle said, "Let's play a game."

Miles winced. "Myrtle, I can't handle any Scrabble right now. And I'm not sure that would be Wanda's forte, either."

Myrtle said, "No, no. We'll play cards. You have cards here, I know. Wanda, you like playing cards, don't you?"

Wanda shrugged a thin shoulder. "Don't reckon I know any games. I only handle tarot cards."

"It'll be easy. We can teach you canasta," said Myrtle briskly.

Miles was already shaking his head. "Too complicated, Myrtle."

"All right then, hearts."

Miles shook his head again. "We'd spend half the time trying to explain the game. And I might need a refresher on hearts, myself."

"Fine! Although I have to say that you have no sense of adventure whatsoever. We can do crazy eights, old maid, or go fish. And don't you dare tell me that those are too complex. Little Jack can play those like a card shark and he's only in preschool," said Myrtle.

Myrtle pulled out the cards and shuffled them thoroughly. She started dealing them out and Wanda watched her as she did. Miles reluctantly sat down at the kitchen table. "We might need more coffee," he muttered. "So what game are we playing?"

"Crazy eights. It's mindless," said Myrtle. "Wanda, the eights are wild."

Wanda gave Myrtle a baffled look.

Miles added, "You can make the eights anything that you like. So hearts, diamonds, spades, etc."

Wanda looked worried. "What are them?"

"Did you never play cards, then?" Myrtle looked stunned. "That's a pity. All right, watch Miles and me play for a while. Sit where you can see my cards and I'll whisper to you what I'm trying to do and what my strategy is."

Miles said, "Or we could just do an example round and put both of our hands on the table so that she can see them."

"But that takes the fun out of it! I'm trying to beat you . . . that's the fun." And Myrtle rapidly did, explaining the game to Wanda all the while and pointing out the names of the different cards.

The next game Wanda decided hesitantly that she might want her own hand. She did and won.

"Beginner's luck?" asked Miles, looking surprised. "Was she dealt a hand of eights?"

Myrtle said, "Wanda catches on fast."

After Wanda won the following three games, Myrtle said, "Now Wanda. You know I have to ask this question. As a psychic, you're not able to *know* what our cards are, are you?"

"That ain't the way—" started Wanda.

"I know—the way the sight works." But Myrtle still gave her a suspicious look.

Miles the Peacemaker said, "It's time for more snacks."

Myrtle snorted. "At this rate, we won't be able to *leave* your house, Miles. You'll have to roll us out of here."

Still, she acquiesced. And so, when Red finally returned after some time, they were all still in the kitchen with the remains of a sandwich buffet of ham, tomatoes, and peanut butter and jelly in front of them.

"Well, tell us!" said Myrtle imperiously as they stood up. "We've been waiting here forever."

Red shook his head, seemingly having a tough time finding the words. "The dogs found her right away."

Myrtle put a hand to her heart. "That poor girl."

Miles still seemed to be having a tough time wrapping his head around it all. "So, they went right to it?"

"I was going to lead them right to the area Wanda described, but the dogs got there before I could even do that," said Red.

"And it's definitely Tara?" asked Miles.

Red said with a shrug, "I reckon. I mean, the state police will have their guy take a look and identify. But with what Wanda here said, I can't figure it could be anybody else. Of course, the state guys were real keen for me to tell them who I thought the anonymous informant was."

He gave Wanda a hard look, and she gave him a tired one in return.

Myrtle said fiercely, "Well, you can't. They'll never understand, the Philistines. Besides, it doesn't matter how she was found, it only matters that she was *found*. I suppose you'll be giving her poor parents some closure with the news."

He sighed. "Once we track them down. They left town some time ago."

"How on earth were they able to keep this a secret for so long?" asked Miles. "Wouldn't someone have noticed a big dug-up area in the yard? Or is the entire Epps family in on it?"

Red said, "I hadn't remembered this myself, but one of the neighbors who came out to see what we were doing mentioned that around the time Tara disappeared, they were installing a sewer line on the street."

Myrtle said, "So they just chucked the body in there? And no one ever noticed?"

Red shrugged, "I guess they were finished with that section. The fact of the matter is that it would have been really loose soil. It wouldn't have been much effort to dig some dirt back out, conceal a body, and cover it back up." He gave Wanda a serious stare. "You're absolutely sure that you don't have any other information about this?"

Wanda looked down at her scuffed shoes and silently shook her head.

Myrtle asked, "What did Hubert say?"

"Well, he wasn't any too pleased about us bringing dogs in. But let's face it—he thought he was settled in for a quiet night with a six-pack of beer and a couple of TV shows. Instead, we discover a body on his property. And right away," said Red.

"Was he cooperative?" asked Miles.

"He seemed pretty stunned when we told him we'd found a body and that we thought it was Tara. Then he shut up real quick." He looked at his mother. "Now, I know that you have some sort of theory about all of this. I have the feeling that you're not even all that surprised that Tara's body was at Hubert Epps's house."

Myrtle hesitated. She never liked sharing information with Red, but she didn't mind bragging just a little about what she'd found out so far. She said cautiously, "Well, I'm not really. I've heard that Boone was dating Tara and Rose was arguing with Tara. And they had that big party and I suppose things got out of hand, although I've no idea who's actually responsible for the poor girl's death."

Red frowned. "Boone was not dating Tara."

Chapter Seventeen

Myrtle said, "I heard that he was."

Red said, "Well, I remember that they *weren't*. Boone *wanted* to date Tara. Honestly, if it were today and he was hounding her like he was, she'd probably have put some kind of restraining order on him."

Myrtle sat back in her chair. "Is that so? And I thought he was supposed to be some sort of heartthrob. That all the girls wanted to go out with Boone."

Red shrugged. "That might be the case overall, but Tara sure didn't want to. And she didn't have to! She was a beautiful girl and she could have gone out with anybody that she wanted to. But the truth of the matter is that, looking back, she simply wasn't ready to start dating. And that only seemed to make Boone more determined than ever to go out with her. In fact, he was going around spreading rumors they *were* going out."

Miles asked, "He was pursuing the one thing he couldn't have?"

"Exactly. He was sort of spoiled, I always thought, both by his daddy and his mama. Rotten. And he got away with it because he was so charming when he got caught out. You know they found out about this party that was going on," said Red to his mother.

Myrtle said, "So there *was* a party."

"There was. Again, one that I didn't attend," said Red, rolling his eyes.

Myrtle said, "Well, I'm certainly glad to hear that I'd raised you well. You knew that I wouldn't have wanted you to go to a party when the parents weren't in attendance."

Red said dryly, "I'm happy you're ascribing my absence there to my wonderful upbringing, but the fact of the matter is that I had a football game to play in."

Myrtle felt somewhat deflated. "Oh. Okay, so tell me what happened when Hubert and Pearl came back into town."

"From what I'd heard at the time—and we'll be covering all this again in interviews—Boone and Rose did their best to clean up the house and the property. There were beer bottles and plastic cups and cigarette butts and things like that everywhere. Plus, folks had pulled out food from the fridge, eaten on it, and left it in various degrees of going rotten," said Red. "They worked hard cleaning it all up."

Miles said, "To the extent that they or a party guest also cleaned up the evidence of a body and concocted a story about Tara running away."

"Well, somebody did," said Red.

Miles said hesitantly, "May I ask a question on a completely different subject, Red?"

Red raised his eyebrows in surprise. "Well, sure thing, Miles. You look like you have something on your mind."

"It's just—have you seen Elaine this evening? I mean, before all the finding-Tara business happened? I know you've been busy with the case," said Miles.

Myrtle snorted. "I have a feeling I know what this is regarding."

Apparently Red did too, because his face lit up with a big grin. "As a matter of fact, I surely did. And she showed me some delightful pictures from a soiree you hosted earlier today."

Myrtle said, "It's not a soiree if it isn't at night. It was simply . . . a rather rowdy gathering."

"Well, I could tell that everybody was having a lot of fun, that's for sure. And to think that I believed book club was a stuffy group! I never knew what y'all were really up to. I thought everybody was discussing literature." Red chuckled.

Myrtle said, "We *rarely* discuss literature unless Miles or I have been able to choose. What Elaine pictured today was a very unusual club meeting."

Miles cleared his throat. "What I was wondering is, if she and Sloan were planning on *running* those pictures in the paper. That is, I thought perhaps the events tonight might preclude lighthearted photos from being published."

Red crinkled his brow. "I think the paper's policy is to run all sorts of stories each day. Some sad stories, some purely informational, some that would qualify as fluff pieces."

"Book club would definitely fall under the fluff category," said Myrtle.

Miles said, "Maybe it will just run on the social media site."

Wanda croaked, "Runnin' in the paper."

Miles looked startled. "You mean that . . . you *know* that? You saw it in some sort of vision or something?"

Wanda shook her head tiredly. "Nope. Done talked to Sloan on the phone earlier. He tol' me then."

Miles slumped in his chair.

Red stood up. "All right. I'd better head out. Now I've got a cold case *and* a couple of recent homicides on my hands." He glanced over at Wanda. "Wanda, I'd be happy to drive you back home."

Myrtle said, "I'll drive her back."

Red raised his eyebrows. "I don't care how well you fancy you drive, Mama. The sun is going down and you are in a loaned car. Loaned, as a matter of fact, by a suspect in a murder investigation."

"Who is innocent until proven guilty," said Myrtle. "And I'm perfectly capable of getting Wanda back home safely."

"Regardless, I'd like to do the honor," said Red firmly. He smiled broadly at Wanda and she gave him a tentative smile in response as she stood up and walked out with him.

"Blast!" said Myrtle, thumping her hand on Miles's table and making him jump. "Red is getting all into my business. And where is Dusty with those gnomes? Red is really overstepping the line."

Miles said mildly, "Frankly, I'm not much of one for driving at night, myself. As far as I'm concerned, he was doing us a favor driving all the way out to the country to take Wanda back home."

"It wasn't simply a kind gesture. He'll be quizzing her all the way home, I bet you." Myrtle fumed.

Miles said, "Aside from that one misstep on Red's part, I thought the evening ended up yielding a good deal of information. We now know that Tara really is dead, for one."

"We already knew that. Wanda mentioned it ages ago," said Myrtle.

"Yes, but now it's confirmed and they've found her. We also found out that Boone simply *wanted* Tara to be his girlfriend. That he even *bragged* that she was his girlfriend. Maybe Georgia Simpson thought they were together because of the amount of time that Tara spent with Boone's sister. But now we know that no matter what Boone said, he and Tara weren't going out at all," said Miles.

Myrtle thought about this. "Yes, but this is completely different information than we'd heard before. Perhaps Red's memory isn't reliable."

Miles said, "He was very matter of fact about it. And I've never known Red's memory to be anything *but* reliable. He's been a police officer his entire life. He lives off his powers of observation."

Myrtle said, "Point taken. But the Epps kids must be involved. I suppose Hubert and Pearl are off the hook, considering that they were both out of town . . . a fact that a slew of partying kids could confirm. Tara's disappearance happened during their party. Boone was clearly fixated on her and she was bent on rejecting him. And she and Rose had an argument . . . I do believe Georgia on that one."

"Perhaps Boone became frustrated when Tara rejected him again," said Miles thoughtfully.

"Maybe. Oh, it's all such a mess. How does it all tie into Pearl's and Nell's deaths?" Myrtle pursed her lips and stared at Miles's ceiling. "I know. It's just like we were saying. Boone is a frustrated paramour. Rose argues with Tara. Tara dies . . . somehow. Pearl finds out and writes a book about it. Now the kids are desperate to cover up the information to stay out of jail!"

Miles nodded. "It does all make sense. Except for the part where Pearl waits for thirty years to finally tell the story. That's what I'm not exactly sure about."

Myrtle sighed. "I know. But maybe Pearl only recently found out about it. Maybe Hubert and she had some sort of plumbing issue and they had to do some digging. Maybe they tried to plant a tree where Tara was buried and they discovered her. Pearl was quite the gardener, you know."

Miles raised his eyebrows. "Such a gardener that she wouldn't 'call before she dug?' If there's a sewer line down there, surely Pearl would have had the town put markers out."

"All right then, maybe she did know about it. Maybe Pearl Epps had this deep, dark secret that she kept hidden for years and years until finally it started eating her up alive and she decided that she simply couldn't keep it anymore," said Myrtle.

Miles sighed. "It certainly seems like the most likely option, looking at all that we know. But it's hard to imagine cheerful, crafty Pearl as someone with a dark, horrid secret. She always reminded me of Minnie Pearl when I looked at her."

"I'll agree with you that it's hard to think of Pearl that way. But let's face it; she said that she was writing that book to disclose some old secrets. The way Pearl was talking, it sounded like she realized that keeping secrets was detrimental to her family.

Like the only way to move forward was to own up to whatever the secret was and go from there," said Myrtle.

"No wonder they were so upset about the book. She would reveal the fact that someone in her family was a killer. That person would obviously go to jail and who knows what would happen to everyone else for covering up a crime? Sounds like it would have meant jail time for everybody," said Miles.

"Right. Pearl got tired of harboring the secret. She stated she's writing a book. No one believed her until the thing was finished and she announced it at a family dinner. The next thing we know, she's been pushed down the stairs and the manuscript is stolen and most likely destroyed."

Miles said, "None of this really explains what happened to Nell, though."

Myrtle shrugged. "Nell knew something. She was a liability."

"Do you think that she also knew about Tara's murder? And her burial in her sister's yard?" asked Miles.

Myrtle considered this for a few seconds and then shook her head. "I doubt it. Nell's not the sort to cover up something like that. She always seemed like a straight arrow to me. No, if Nell had known something about Tara's death, she'd have reported it straight to the police."

Miles said slowly, "So maybe she knew something about Pearl's death."

"Hard to imagine. It looks to me that Pearl was alone with her killer. But maybe Nell somehow *did* know something. Maybe Pearl mentioned to her sister that she was planning on speaking with Boone or Rose that morning. Who knows?

Maybe she really didn't even know anything at all and someone merely *thought* she did and murdered her," said Myrtle.

"What's our next step?" asked Miles.

"Rose," said Myrtle simply. "Edward thinks that she was spending time over at Nell's house. I'd like to know more about it."

"And how do you propose that we go about finding that out? Hover around her dog-walking route?" asked Miles.

"Better than that. Her mother's funeral is tomorrow. I believe that will be an excellent time to catch her," said Myrtle. "And if not, I can deliver this casserole we picked up at the store. Otherwise, I'll have to eat it myself."

The next morning, Myrtle fed Pasha and herself and started getting ready for Pearl's funeral. Fortunately, she had a new funeral outfit. Relatively new, anyway, as it had already been worn on a handful of outings. She still felt rather daring wearing slacks to a funeral since the Southern decree had always been a somber dress and pantyhose with polished shoes.

She glanced at her watch. She hoped that Miles was ready to go. He was supposed to pick her up for the funeral. At this point, she was starting to think she should simply drive herself and leave Miles up to his own devices. Finally, there was a tap at the door.

"There you are!" she fussed, hurrying out the front door.

"I'm only three minutes late," said Miles mildly as he followed her to his car.

"Mark my words, this funeral is going to be standing room only. Pearl was an important figure in this town," said Myrtle, quickly getting into the car and buckling up. "What made you run behind? That's most unlike you."

"The newspaper," said Miles gloomily. "Didn't you see it this morning?"

Myrtle smiled. "You mean the wonderful promotional pictures of the book club? I predict Tippy is going to get a ton of requests from people to join. Everyone looked like they were having such *fun*."

"If that's what you'd prefer to call it," said Miles, face set grimly.

"Think of it as good promo. No one would want to come to book club ordinarily. It's way too crusty and formal," said Myrtle. "Besides, I'm sure no one even noticed the picture of you."

"Me napping," said Miles unhappily.

"As far as anyone could tell, you might simply have been blinking when the photo was taken. Don't worry about it Miles, for heaven's sake. Let's just get to the church before we have to stand in the back."

Sure enough, every pew was packed.

Myrtle sighed. "This is what I was afraid of. We should have been here forty-five minutes ago."

"But you're the one who set the time for me to pick you up," said Miles.

Myrtle said, "Clearly, I didn't really think it through. What a mess. Oh, there's Red. He always stands out with that hair. I never had a hard time picking him out at a sporting event, growing up. Except for football—those helmets didn't help."

"Does *he* have a seat?" asked Miles, sounding hopeful. "He might give it up to us. Maybe the two of us could squeeze into his spot."

"Nope. He's standing." She turned to Miles. "Here, look frail."

Miles stared at her. "Frail? I can't pull that off."

"Sure you can," said Myrtle impatiently. "Here, take my cane. Now lean over it and blink a lot. I'll do my usual doddering old lady act."

"Aren't we blocking everyone, standing in the middle of the church aisle?" murmured Miles.

"Certainly not! We're looking for a spot. Either an usher will come over or some good Samaritans will offer us their seats," said Myrtle. She effected looking exhausted and put out a hand to clutch the end of a pew for support.

A minute later, a strapping young man and his somewhat annoyed-looking wife offered them their seats.

"They didn't look that handicapped to me," Myrtle heard the wife complaining as they walked to the back of the church to stand.

"Don't be silly. They're old folks. I couldn't have slept tonight knowing that I sat while they stood," retorted the young man.

Myrtle and Miles sat in their spots, which were excellent at about five seats from the very front of the church.

"Now, isn't this better?" asked Myrtle smugly, taking her cane back from Miles.

"I suppose. Although my pride is stinging," said Miles.

"We have no idea how long this service will go on. We might as well be comfortable and those young people didn't need to sit down. That's what's wrong with our country—too many people sitting all day long."

Miles said, "So *that's* what's wrong with our country?"

"Exactly. When I was their age, I was standing all day long as a schoolteacher. And I'm sure as an architect, you were standing a lot at building sites," said Myrtle.

Miles gritted through his teeth, "Engineer. I was an engineer."

"Whatever. The point is that they don't need their seats," said Myrtle blithely.

It ended up that it was a good thing that they were both seated. It went on and on. There were hymns to start out with.

"We shouldn't have to sing *all* the verses of each hymn," whispered Miles after a particularly dragging rendition of *How Firm a Foundation, Ye Saints of the Lord*. "Especially when they have six stanzas and the organ part drags a bit."

"It *has* to drag a bit. It was written in 1787. They didn't know *how* to write peppy stuff back then," said Myrtle. "But I agree with you. It seems like an odd choice for Hubert or Boone to have picked out."

Miles whispered gloomily, "I have the feeling that Rose and the minister came up with the service together. She seems the type to pick hymns as a sort of penance." He brightened. "At least we have a shorter one coming up. *Sweet Hour of Prayer*."

"A lovely hymn. But I don't believe it's going to be played at a fast clip here. Or even at its normal pace. The organist is taking her sweet time today," said Myrtle.

And indeed, each note was drawn-out as long as was possible by the organist. Myrtle noticed that Hubert and Boone were looking antsy, restlessly shifting in the pew. Boone pulled at his suit collar as if it were too tight on him.

Miles said, "The program shows one final hymn at the very end. Everything should be speeding up now."

But then the minister, perhaps rather carried away with the huge crowd in the sanctuary, delivered a full twenty-five-minute sermon, mentioning Pearl only in passing as a godly woman.

Even worse, the woman behind them apparently had some sort of dire affliction. Her coughing had been going on since they arrived, but now reached a crescendo. She loudly unwrapped cough drop after cough drop, to no avail. Miles flinched each time she gave her deep, grating, productive cough.

"I'm glad I don't have to worry about germs anymore," he said fervently to Myrtle.

Myrtle gave him a short smile. She had the feeling that Wanda's lie had actually been that Miles *didn't* need to be careful of germs. That Wanda realized Miles was rather incapacitated after her prediction. She turned and glared at the culprit after a particularly wet cough that didn't sound covered.

"Surely we're almost done now," said Miles, studying his church bulletin as if it held the secret to life buried in its text.

"Looks like there are to be readings," said Myrtle. "And then eulogies."

The readings varied from lyrics of rather sappy modern songs to a quotation from Hamlet: "To die, to sleep – to sleep, perchance to dream."

Myrtle snorted. "They can't even get the quotation right. Nor the tone! It's not a happy statement on being dead. They left off the end of the quotation: '– ay, there's the rub, for in this sleep of death what dreams may come...?'"

"Put an F on their paper with your red pen," said Miles mildly. "Come on, it's nearly done. Just the eulogies to go."

But the eulogies ended up taking the most time of all. It appeared every person in Bradley wanted to speak and that none of them had prepared for it. This resulted in rambling and repetitive narratives that frequently veered off the topic of Pearl. Hubert appeared at one point to be nodding off.

Myrtle growled, "We should try escaping."

Miles murmured, "We're so close to the front that we can't really slip out undetected."

"People would understand. We're seniors. Seniors get uncomfortable sitting down for too long and it makes them develop clots. Seniors frequently need to visit the restroom, for heaven's sake. They'd all forgive us and wish that they were seniors themselves and could leave without a fuss," hissed Myrtle.

But then there was a soaring crescendo of organ music indicating the end of the service and the mourners rose to sing one final, and mercifully shorter, hymn. Then it was all over.

"Now we can go," sighed Miles in relief.

Chapter Eighteen

"Go? No, this is precisely when we need to stay. This is when we need to speak with Rose so we don't have to chase her down on the road when she's dog-walking," said Myrtle. "Or give her that casserole. I've a mind to eat it for my supper."

Miles said, "But look at that line. There's a huge line of people waiting to speak to the family."

"We'll stand up and stretch for a few minutes and then we can sit back down again and wait for the church to empty out," said Myrtle.

"Can't we just go to the funeral reception?" asked Miles, sounding hopeful. "We've done that before, haven't we? Spoken to family at the reception?"

"Yes, but never for a funeral that's this big. Most of the town is here. I doubt we'd get an opportunity to even get close to Rose there."

They did stretch and even walked around the sanctuary, pretending interest in the stained-glass windows. An old man slapped Miles heartily on the back, surprising him and nearly sending him through the aforementioned window. The man guffawed and asked, "Did you have fun at book club? Didn't know it was the place to party. And lots of fillies there, too." He gave Miles a big wink. Seeing Myrtle, he winced and politely said, "Heard you've been under the weather, Myrtle. Hope you're better now." He headed on his way. Miles stared miserably after him and Myrtle glowered.

"Imbecile!" hissed Myrtle. "You won't find him at book club because he barely knows how to read."

"Did you teach *him*, too?" asked Miles morosely.

"Certainly not! He's older than you are," said Myrtle. "Look, we can start moving to the front of the church."

Finally, the crowd at the front of the church dwindled and Myrtle and Miles hurried to speak to the family before they left for the reception. Myrtle noted that Red was still there, watching the family from a respectful distance. Rose was already in the pew, gathering her purse.

Myrtle said kindly, "It was a lovely tribute to your mother, Rose."

She was surprised as Rose reached out suddenly and pulled Myrtle in for a hug. Myrtle patted her awkwardly on the back as Rose's muffled voice said, "That means a lot to me since you really knew Mama."

Miles cleared his throat. "The entire town was here to pay their respects. That must make you feel good."

Rose said, "If *anything* can make me feel good right now. It's been such a horrid week. And now we'll have to plan a service for Aunt Nell! I didn't think I'd ever have to figure out two services in a week. And of course, I can't just copy what we did for

Mama because she and Nell were so different. What worked for Mama won't work for Nell."

Miles looked vastly relieved at this pronouncement, having no apparent desire to repeat the past hour and a half.

Myrtle said, "I'm sure you'll come up with something simple and splendid. I'm just so sorry about your poor aunt."

Rose nodded. "It's such a shock. I mean, Mama's death was a shock, but then to have Nell's on top of it all?" She sighed. "And I had just seen her. Not that that means anything, really. But it made it that much harder for me to get it through my head that she is actually gone."

"Oh, that's lovely that you could see her before she passed. Was it in the last couple of days then?" asked Myrtle in her best concerned old-lady voice.

Rose quickly said, "Oh, I really hadn't *seen* her, seen her. I only meant to say that I'd run by her house to help her change a lightbulb that was difficult to access. I *wish* that I'd had a real visit with Nell, but I didn't. The night she died I was out walking dogs. Tippy's dogs, actually. She's been out of town for a little while," said Rose.

Miles winced at the mention of Tippy's absence, which apparently brought to mind the general debauchery of the book club meeting.

Rose's eyes were huge in her face. Then she blurted, "I'm wondering if Edward might have done it. Oh, I don't know! That sounds so wicked to say that I can't even believe that the words left my mouth! Don't listen to me. I haven't slept for days and I don't know what I'm saying."

Myrtle said gently, "But sometimes that's when the truth is easier to discern. Something must have made you say that. What was it?"

Rose glanced around her fearfully as if Edward might be lurking in a pew somewhere. Then she said, "He and Nell had a huge argument recently. Nell was really upset about it and didn't want to see Edward at all. I mean, it was just a tiff, but her feelings were definitely hurt."

"Any idea what they might have been arguing about?" asked Miles.

Rose sighed. "Edward wanted to marry Nell and Nell wanted to stay independent. Nell always said that she had no intention of marrying. She liked doing things her own way and she could be very hardheaded."

Miles said, "Well, after spending so many years by herself, it would be hard to try to adjust your schedule to someone else's."

Rose nodded. "There's that. And Nell liked her house just-so. She didn't like the idea of Edward coming in and leaving newspapers on the floor or taking off his socks and not putting them in the hamper. She just preferred to be by herself and not have someone living with her. She liked going out to see a matinee movie with Edward or to go out to lunch with him, but when all was said and done, she wanted to keep to herself."

Myrtle said, "Makes sense to me. Who wants to train a man at this point in our lives? But Edward didn't see it that way, apparently?"

Rose shook her head. "I guess that's one thing that they both had in common—being hardheaded. Edward was determined to convince Nell that she needed to marry him. He told her that they'd have this wonderful, romantic life together and could travel and stuff."

Myrtle said, "I've never noticed Nell going on too many trips. She seems like a homebody to me."

"That's exactly it. She likes to stay at home, or at least in Bradley. She volunteers at the church and then she tinkers around her house. She had quite a routine, and she wasn't going to be convinced by Edward to make changes," said Rose.

Miles said slowly, "He seemed really devoted to Nell. But is he the kind of guy who could lose his temper and commit murder simply by being frustrated?"

Rose shrugged, looking uncomfortable. "I don't know what to say to that. I really don't want to get Edward into any trouble. There isn't any hard evidence or anything like that, either. Just a gut feeling. My gut says *maybe*."

Myrtle decided that Rose's gut was decidedly wishy-washy.

Seeing Myrtle's steady gaze, Rose elaborated weakly, "Edward did lose his temper at the family dinner when Mama announced her book was finished and ready for editing."

Myrtle pressed her lips together. Clearly there would be no more forthcoming information regarding Edward since they'd known about Edward's blow-up at dinner since the very beginning. She said instead, feeling that the element of surprise could be on her side, "On another subject, I heard from Red about what happened at your father's house last night. I'm just so sorry."

Rose trembled. "I know. I don't know what happened. We all thought that Tara had run away from home." She shook her head and said almost to herself. "I feel terrible. Like it's my fault."

Myrtle said gently, "Well, I remember teaching young Tara, and I thought at the time that she wasn't much of a candidate for running away. She was a high-performing student who seemed to have friends and a very stable home life."

Rose said in a broken voice, "The worst thing is that she and I argued the night she disappeared. I hate that was the last time I ever saw her."

Myrtle noticed that Hubert was looking their way with narrowed eyes. But she also noticed that he was talking with Erma Sherman. And Erma, for all her many faults, was impossible to get away from.

Myrtle continued, "It was high school, Rose. These kinds of arguments happen in high school because half the population is petty and the other half likes drama. Do you remember what the argument was about?"

Rose took a deep, shaky breath and then moistened her lips. She said, "Nothing. It was about nothing. I didn't get on the cheer squad and Tara did. That's all. Petty, like you said."

Miles glanced at Myrtle and gave a small shrug. It sounded like the type of argument a teenage girl might have.

Myrtle said slowly, "I heard that Boone wanted to date Tara and was rebuffed. I remember how close you and your brother were back then. You weren't upset with Tara over not dating Boone, were you?"

Rose's face again streaked with color.

Bingo, thought Myrtle.

She stuttered, "Nope, it was just a silly argument. I wish it hadn't happened now and I'm so, so sorry that she's dead. Miss Myrtle, I need to go now and get ready for the funeral reception."

With that, she bolted for the sanctuary door that led out to the restrooms.

Myrtle gave Miles a look. Miles murmured, "Let's talk about it when we leave."

As they turned around, Boone Epps called out in a jaunty voice that didn't fit their surroundings, "Hey, Miss Myrtle! You gonna keep that car or you wanna trade it for something else? You know that I won't be happy until you're happy."

Myrtle saw Red glaring across the church.

Myrtle smiled broadly at him. "I hate to bother you on a day like this, Boone."

He raised his eyebrows. "Don't worry about that! A man's gotta eat, right? I'm going to work right after we're done with the funeral today. Believe me, I need the distraction and work is the *perfect* distraction . . . unless we're too quiet."

Hubert interjected, "He's at that dealership *all* the time. Very, very early in the morning and very late at night."

Myrtle said, "I completely understand. In that case, I'll see you this afternoon."

Myrtle hopped in the car with Miles. "Well, what did you think of *that*?"

Miles said, "I thought it was the most unnecessarily long funeral service I've ever had to sit through. I'm glad Rose won't repeat it with Nell. And I'm delighted you don't want to go to the reception."

"Did I say that?" asked Myrtle, frowning. "I believe I simply said that we wouldn't be able to talk with the *family* at the reception."

"If you skip the reception," said Miles in a desperate tone, "then I will pay for your lunch."

Myrtle swung around in the front seat. "Really? Will you? I don't think you've ever paid for my lunch, Miles."

"Extraordinary times call for extraordinary measures," said Miles grimly. He paused. "I'm assuming that you'll take advantage of this situation by choosing a nice restaurant?"

"Certainly not! I'm still craving the Bo's Diner special. Let's go there. It'll be completely dead since the entire town appears to be at the funeral reception," said Myrtle.

It was, indeed, dead there as they discovered minutes later. They found a parking spot right in the front and walked right to a table. They were served in no time as the whole staff seemed to have been waiting on them to arrive, thrilled to have something to do.

"Now," said Myrtle, pushing back her empty plate. "On to the Rose revelation."

Miles frowned and took a last bite of his three-bean salad. "Remind me what the Rose revelation was again? I'd gotten the impression that she was fibbing during our conversation."

"Precisely! She acted as if she and Tara had been arguing over the cheer squad," said Myrtle with a snort.

Miles shrugged. "It sounded like a perfectly reasonable explanation to me, considering what little I remember of high school. High school was definitely a place where cheerleading was a big deal."

"A big deal to some people. It probably was a big deal in terms of status to *Boone*. But Rose never cared a bit about cheerleading. She wasn't the most coordinated of girls. Rose was never on the cheer squad and I don't think she likely ever even tried out. Did you notice how Rose changed color when I mentioned the possibility that the argument was over Boone's hope to date Tara? I thought Rose would pass out for a moment," said Myrtle.

Miles said, "So Boone and Rose were close enough back then that Rose cared who he dated? They don't seem that close now."

"Now they're both adults and have different lives. But Boone still seems rather protective of Rose."

Miles said, "Not as much as Hubert is protective of her."

Myrtle said, "The secrets are causing the problems, don't you see? Pearl was right. This family has too many secrets and too many alliances. It's far too complex." She glanced at her watch. "Do you think the reception is over now and we can go to the car dealership to see Boone? Or should we linger here some more?"

Miles groaned. "The dealership again. Now what, Myrtle? A yellow car?"

"Don't be silly. I've decided that I don't want a car after all."

"What?" Miles's eyes were big.

"That's right. Who wants the trouble? Gas prices are up and down all the time. I'd have to worry about oil changes and tire rotations and flats. No, it's much better to ask others for rides. And now Red is aware of the situation and may clear his calendar better to provide me with trips to the store. I'll tell Boone that and thank him for his time," said Myrtle.

"Now that you got the reaction from Red that you wanted?" asked Miles, rolling his eyes.

"He deserved it. He acts as if I'm incapable of doing *anything*. It's all very annoying," said Myrtle.

Miles said, "My only suggestion? Don't tell Boone that you're not buying a car until *after* we've finished talking with him."

Myrtle wagged a finger at him. "Good point. Besides, I have a plan. First off, let's get the black car and I'll follow you over to the dealership to return it."

Chapter Nineteen

The car dealership was as dead as the diner had been with most of the town apparently taking naps after all the food at the funeral reception. As Boone had promised, however, he was there. He spotted them from the showroom and raised a hand in greeting.

Miles sighed. "I'm not really looking forward to this."

"We simply need to find more information now that Tara's body has been found. It's not that big of a deal," said Myrtle.

"He didn't seem very big on disclosing information last time," said Miles.

"Well, now a body has been found on his father's property. A property where Boone used to live. And it's the body of a girl that Boone had a big crush on. He should expect some questions about it," said Myrtle. She saw Miles make a face. "Just pretend to be on your phone if you get uncomfortable this time. You don't have to be part of our conversation."

"Miss Myrtle!" Boone swept up to her and gave her a peck on the cheek. "Thank you so much for coming to Mama's service today. You know she would have appreciated you being there."

"Where else would I have been?" asked Myrtle. "Your mama was a dear, sweet lady. Of course I wanted to be there to show my respect for her."

Boone clapped his hands together. "Now, on to business. What are we going to do about the car?"

Miles looked anxiously at Myrtle. Myrtle, who hadn't expected Boone to lead with the car thing immediately, quickly said, "We're going to all be irritated at Red. Red doesn't want me to have a car and he's been hassling me about it since I started test-driving different models. Yes, it's all Red's fault."

Miles hid a smile. Throwing Red under the bus was probably the best option. After all, it was the truth that he didn't want Myrtle to own a car, even if Myrtle wouldn't have let that stop her if she'd really wanted one. And considering the fact that Boone was a murder suspect several times over, Boone wasn't likely to confront Red over the matter.

Boone made a face. "Aw. I'm sorry to hear that, Miss M. It sure don't seem fair. *Doesn't* seem fair," he corrected hastily. "But I totally understand."

Now he was looking up at the showroom again as if wanting very much to be back up there and continuing whatever it was that he'd been doing.

Myrtle said, "What's not fair is what your family is going through. It sure seems like when it rains, it pours, doesn't it? First your mother, then your aunt, and now poor Tara."

Miles pulled his phone out and started messing with various apps.

Boone got very still for a couple of seconds as if trying to decide what was the right response. He finally said, "Reckon you heard about that from Red. But we don't know whose body it is. For all we know, it could be some sort of historical discovery from two hundred years ago."

"Red didn't seem to think so. No, it sounded as if the body belonged to that poor girl." Myrtle paused. She tilted her head to one side as if trying to dredge up an old memory. "Now, that was a long time ago but do I remember correctly that you used to date her?"

Boone shook his head and gave a short laugh. "Nope. You've gotten me mixed up with some other student, Miss Myrtle. Tara and I never did go out. In fact, Tara looked down her nose at most boys. She thought we were all uncouth. Maybe we were. Anyway, she was more into her cheerleading and her Future Business Leaders of America club and whatever else smart-kid stuff she was doing. If it is Tara in Dad's yard, I don't have a clue what she's doing there."

Miles said, "But wasn't she at your party?"

For a moment, Boone's expression was unguarded and he shot an annoyed look at Miles. Miles quickly toyed with his phone again.

Myrtle said, "Good point, Miles. Shouldn't you have known what she's doing there if she ended up in your dad's yard the night of your party?"

Boone was already backing up and moving toward the showroom and offices. "I had lots of parties, y'all. Mama and Daddy went out of town every chance they got back then. Maybe I wasn't so well-supervised, you know? You should take that up with Daddy. Now I understand about the car, Miss M, but now that we know we're done, I gotta take care of some business that really *might* lead to a sale. See you later." In his haste to get away, he dropped a pen that he was carrying and Miles stooped to pick it up and handed it to him.

Myrtle and Miles got into Miles's car. "All right," said Myrtle. "Well, he was definitely not being helpful. He was, in fact, obfuscating."

"Shouldn't he be? Isn't that the natural reaction when someone is hinting that you might be responsible for three deaths?" asked Miles as he drove away from the parking lot.

"You'd think he'd be more like his mother and realize that secrets aren't healthy," said Myrtle. She paused. "Where are you heading?"

"Home," he said simply. "It's time."

"It's time for us to talk to Hubert," said Myrtle. "We can even stop by the store and pick up a quiche to bring with us. Because I'm going to keep Rose's casserole for myself."

"He has enough food to last him for weeks after that funeral reception. You know it must have been loaded with food."

Myrtle said, "But the entire town was there. And the entire town eats a lot of food. He might be able to use a homemade quiche."

"Homemade?"

"Homemade by somebody," snapped Myrtle.

Miles said, "I think we should leave Hubert alone. He has had a rough twenty-four hours between finding a body found in his yard and the death of his wife. He probably wants to hide indoors and lick his wounds."

"Precisely why we should visit him now. He'll be off-balance and unguarded and may actually provide information about Tara or Pearl or Nell or all of them," said Myrtle.

Miles shook his head. "I don't want to. Plus, I'm starting to get a massive headache. The last thing I need is to go grocery shopping for quiches or harass widowers. Let's go tomorrow morning. After a good night's sleep, this headache should be gone." He pulled up to Myrtle's house. "Someone has been hard at work."

And indeed, the yard was covered by Myrtle's gnomes. Every inch of the front yard had a gnome in it.

Myrtle frowned. "Usually he doesn't put them *all* in the front yard. Ordinarily, he'd scatter some of them in the side yards where they're still visible." Her eyes narrowed. "I have the sinking sensation that he's trying to kill my grass so he doesn't have to cut it."

"Good luck with that," said Miles. "I'll see you tomorrow."

Myrtle changed from her funeral clothes finally to something more casual. Then she took her cane and set off for a walk to clear her head and forget about dying grass and gnomes before she looked for something in the house to eat for supper. Besides, there was something she wanted to see at Hubert's house.

When Myrtle walked up, she saw that Hubert was out in his yard watching a crew of state police going in and out of an incident tent they'd put over a portion of the yard. He raised a hand to wave at her as she stopped. It was the kind of wave you give when you really don't think that the person is planning on coming over.

Myrtle was happy to defy expectations. She raised her hand in response and walked right up to join him.

"You're having a very long day," she said. She gestured to the team of police who appeared to be combing through a pile of dirt. "I'm sorry about all this."

Hubert said, "I hate this, you know." His eyes were bloodshot. "I didn't sleep a wink last night with all the cops and dogs here. And it looks like tonight is going to be more of the same. The neighbors are trying not to look at my yard—at least, not so that I'm seeing them do it. I'm sure when they're behind their curtains, they're watching the show."

Myrtle said, "It sure seemed like everyone at the funeral today was trying to speak with you."

Hubert shrugged. "That's different. They were paying their respects to Pearl. Everyone loved her." He sighed and rubbed his eyes, something that was likely not going to make them any less-bloodshot. "The thing is that I loved her, too. I feel bad that I didn't tell Pearl that more when she was alive. You always feel like you've got tomorrow and sometimes you just don't."

"There are never any guarantees," said Myrtle nodding. "But most of the time we don't expect our loved ones to be taken before their time like Pearl and Nell were. And Tara."

Hubert was quiet, staring at the ground. He glanced over at the police. "You know that I was away that weekend with Pearl. I wish I hadn't been, now. Maybe none of this would have happened." He looked steadily at Myrtle. "You know that my kids had nothing to do with this. They were too busy being host and hostess at the party."

Myrtle resisted the urge to say that Hubert was making it sound like some sort of elegant soiree instead of a keg party thrown by kids whose parents were out of town. Boone and Rose were hardly ensuring the catering staff were passing around the canapés. She said instead, "I'm sure they were."

Hubert, feeling encouraged, continued. "It was probably one of the other kids at the party. You know what high schoolers are like."

"I do indeed, having taught them for so long," said Myrtle. She didn't ask any questions, considering the fact that Hubert was doing an excellent job volunteering information and ideas about what happened.

"Maybe one of the kids was drinking too much and started arguing with Tara," he eagerly continued. "Maybe he didn't mean to, but pushed at her or something. Maybe she hit her head real hard. She wasn't but a little thing."

"Maybe so," said Myrtle noncommittally.

Hubert rubbed his face again. "This whole thing is such a mess. Can't even pay respect to the dead without more stuff happening. You know who I blame for all this?" He looked at Myrtle with his bloodshot eyes. "Edward Hammond."

"You blame him how?" asked Myrtle. "Not for Tara, I wouldn't think. Since it was most unlikely that he was at that party." The last was in a tone of asperity, regardless of her attempt to make it level.

He gave her a hasty glance. "No, not for Tara. Unless there's something I don't know," he said in a hopeful voice. "But for Pearl and for Nell? I totally do. He must have done them both in. Who else could it have been?"

There are none so blind as those who will not see. Myrtle pursed her lips together.

Hubert hurried on. "Anyway, here we are. It's a total mess. I've been a wreck. Since Pearl has been gone, I've been drinking too much, eating just awful, and sleeping day and night. Today was the first day that I felt a little more human." He snorted. "Isn't that crazy? On the day of my wife's funeral, I'm finally able to pull myself together. I got up early even though I didn't sleep much last night. Then I ate pretty well this morning, went to the service, went to the reception, and came back home."

Myrtle said, "Maybe it's because the funeral is allowing you some closure."

Hubert said, "Maybe. Or maybe I just needed something to provide a framework for my day. I'm retired, so I don't have a job to fill the void. And I haven't been the most disciplined guy. But today felt good. So I'll try to get some sleep tonight." He snorted. "Might not happen. But I'm going to give it a go. Then I'll meet up with Boone early tomorrow and we'll have breakfast together at the diner. Get the day started off right. Then maybe I'll take a stroll after that. Just get some structure for my days."

Myrtle nodded. "That's what I do. The sleeping part, not so much. But I do like structure for my day."

Hubert was still watching the police with a worried expression on his face.

Myrtle said, "I'd better be on my way. Take care, Hubert."

Later, as Myrtle stared at the ceiling of her bedroom, she decided that it was definitely *not* a good night's sleep, at least not for her. She had the feeling that Miles might be experiencing the same thing. After very busy days it could be hard to wind down.

She looked at the clock for the fiftieth time and saw it was nearing five. Myrtle got out of bed, dressed, and ate breakfast. Pasha pressed her furry face on the other side of her kitchen window and Myrtle let her in and gave her a can of cat food, which she happily inhaled. She jumped on the windowsill to ask to go out again and Myrtle acquiesced.

Then Myrtle set out for Miles's house with her cane in hand.

It looked as if the lights were out at Miles's, but Myrtle had also known times when he'd been awake and just sitting in the house with the lights off. She rang the doorbell. And waited. Apparently, Miles was *not* awake.

She was turning around with a sigh when she heard the sound of the front door being unlocked. Miles was standing there, bleary-eyed and perspiring.

"You look awful, Miles!" said Myrtle.

He didn't motion her in. "I feel awful. I must have picked up something from the funeral today. Those people were coughing behind us and probably contaminated me."

"It was way too fast to get sick from *that*. It hasn't even been twenty-four hours. It must have been that crazy book club meeting. You know what this means? Dear Wanda lied about lying to you about the germs! She *wanted* you to continue sleuthing with me instead of being worried about getting sick," said Myrtle. "Maybe she needed you with me at the funeral or at the dealership."

Miles said sullenly, "Maybe 'dear Wanda' wanted me sick for some other reason. A reason yet to be revealed."

"Why Miles! It almost sounds as if you believe in her gifts!"

"Only because I'm feverish and delusional. Things are not going well. Not only am I extremely ill, but I've lost my new phone as well," said Miles miserably.

Myrtle said, "It's lucky for you that I happen to be an expert at finding lost things. All we have to do is retrace your steps and we're sure to find it."

"I don't really feel up to doing that," said Miles, clutching at his stomach as if it were about to detonate.

"You're lucky *again* that I spent most of the day with you and I can retrace your steps all by myself." Myrtle paused for a few minutes. She leaned on her cane as she thought and Miles leaned on the front door. Finally, she said, "I've got it. It must be at the car dealership."

Miles considered this. "You know, you might be right. I stooped to pick up Boone's pen and I believe I put my phone down on the hood of a car to reach it."

"I'll simply head over there now and pick it up," said Myrtle carelessly.

Miles's face was horrified. "You can't do that. It's not even dawn! The dealership will be closed. You might even get arrested for trespassing."

Myrtle pointed behind her. "Dawn is breaking now. Besides, there aren't any fences at the dealership. I can simply walk in. I'll need to take your car, of course. Boone may even be there. Hubert said at the funeral that Boone is always at the dealership and he also said that he might join him for an early breakfast today."

Miles sighed and then disappeared into his house for a minute. He returned with car keys, which he thrust at Myrtle.

"Thanks. I'll just let myself in when I come back and will stick your phone on the coffee table. You won't even have to get up."

"Thanks," said Miles rather ungraciously. He gently closed the door and then locked it.

Myrtle pulled up to the dealership and then drove inside the grounds. Although it was deserted, it was brightly lit. She slowly drove to the area where she and Miles had been talking with Boone. Sure enough, Miles's phone was sitting right on top of a white sedan. She parked the car and slid the phone into her purse.

As she was driving back to the entrance, she saw that the lights were also on in the showroom, clearly visible through the glass walls. What was more, she saw that Boone was sitting, crouched over a computer at one of the desks lining the showroom walls.

Myrtle decided she would go in and chat for a few minutes. Tell him that she was also a fellow insomniac—because why else would Boone be at the dealership this early?—and inform him that she'd picked up Miles's phone.

She parked close to the showroom and then walked to the door. When she got there, she paused. Boone was intently looking at a very old, clunky laptop with stickers on the outside. Exactly how Pearl had described her computer.

Myrtle's eyes opened wide and she hastily turned toward Miles's car.

But it was too late. "Miss Myrtle?" drawled Boone's laconic voice behind her.

Chapter Twenty

Myrtle slowly turned around. There was no way she'd be able to outrun Boone. And Boone wasn't going to allow her to pull up the phone app and dial 911. But she did manage to hit a button on Miles's new phone.

"I always said you were a sharp old lady. Of course, back in school, I thought you were old *then*, and you were just a few years older than I am now. And here you are, sharp as a tack, in your 80s. Will wonders never cease?" He grinned at her, but his eyes were hard as flint.

Myrtle gave him a reproving look. It hadn't worked in high school and it didn't seem to be working now, either. "Sharp? In what way? The fact that I found Miles's phone that he lost here earlier? *That* was fairly sharp of me; retracing his steps and then coming here to retrieve the phone."

Boone slowly shook his head. "Nope. You can't pull one over on me, Miss M. Maybe you did come out here to get the phone, but your face a minute ago told me that you realized something. Didn't you? You can't deny it."

Myrtle shrugged. "All right. It looks like you're on your mother's laptop. It was as good a place to keep it as any, wasn't it?

I suppose you had it here the whole time and then you've been keeping odd hours so that you can read her book. Even though you knew what the book would say. That you killed Tara Blanton, hid her body, and then went on your merry way pretending that nothing was wrong. Because that's the kind of person you are—you're tough. But it's nearly killed Rose, hasn't it?"

Boone just stared at her with that fixed grin.

She cleared her throat. "But your plan was quixotic."

Boone snorted. "I never was good at English, Miss M. Remember?"

"Unrealistic. Impractical. Somebody, somewhere, sometime, would find Tara. And somebody did," said Myrtle. "And what happened to your mother and your aunt all dates back to what happened to Tara. Here's what I've heard. You *wanted* to date Tara, but she didn't much want to date you, did she?" She walked toward Boone, into the showroom.

He stepped back a little, reflexively, then leaned casually against the wall, blocking the door. "She didn't really know me."

"You decided to persuade her to date you at the party you and Rose were throwing. But she still wasn't interested. And, thinking on it, you two had nothing in common, Boone. You were a partier, an extrovert. Somebody who was very loud and outgoing. Tara was quieter and more studious. So what was the attraction for you? Just her looks? When she rejected you again, you must have really lost it," said Myrtle.

Boone shrugged. "It was all an accident. There was nothing violent going on that night. You're making it sound like some crazy party . . . like your book club." He gave an unpleasant grin. "Instead, it was pretty tame. We played the radio and drank a little. And yeah, when Tara turned me down, I was a little intoxicated. I might have pushed her some. Because the beer made me more uncoordinated than I usually am, I pushed her harder than I thought. It was just bad luck, Miss M. Just rotten, bad luck."

Myrtle backed a couple of steps into the showroom. Boone didn't move at all. She said, "So when Tara stumbled backward, she fell into something and hit her head wrong. Is that what you're saying, Boone? Did you panic then? Shut the party down? It would have been hard to bury someone with a party going on."

"She wasn't breathing. I tried to do some CPR on her, but she was gone. And no, I didn't panic," said Boone shortly.

"No, you wouldn't have. Rose would have, wouldn't she? Has Rose been the problem all along?" asked Myrtle. "Because that's when the big change happened with Rose, didn't it? I'd thought that she'd argued with Tara because Tara was rebuffing you, but she really was arguing with her about something petty, wasn't she? And she's always felt guilty. That's when she turned into a shadow of herself. You were the one who did that to her by forcing her to lie to the police and lie to Tara's poor family."

"Lie?" drawled Boone.

"That's right. The two of you told everyone that Tara said she wanted to run away. But Tara didn't. Tara never went *anywhere* except right in your parents' yard. And at that point, luck was in your favor because the city was connecting your street to the sewer line. All that ground was dug up, and it was easy to conceal a body and cover it back up with the dirt. But that's also where you were being quixotic again, Boone," said Myrtle.

"Was I? Let's see . . . unrealistic? Is that it?"

"Exactly. Because the workers should have found her. But they didn't. Apparently, they were right at the point of the project where they'd laid the pipe and hadn't covered it all up. You were lucky," said Myrtle. She gasped dramatically and gaped, pointing, into the darkness outside the showroom. "Red?"

Boone turned and Myrtle hurried to the showroom display car and pulled the door handle, praying that the car was unlocked. It was, and she jumped into the driver's seat, locking the doors behind her.

Boone walked up to the car and shook his head, laughing. In a loud voice that could be heard inside the car, he said, "You're something else, Miss Myrtle! And you sure are making a lot of assumptions."

But Myrtle was already busily making phone calls. Boone would have the keys to the car, considering he was a dealer.

Red blearily answered the phone. "What's wrong, Mama?"

"Boone is holding me hostage in the dealership showroom! Bring guns!"

"Whaaaat?"

Myrtle hung up and blared the car horn in long bursts. Maybe it would drive Boone away. Or maybe some irate neighbor would come over.

Boone was now striding over to a small hallway that likely housed his office. Myrtle hopped out of the car and rushed out the door . . . and straight into the arms of Hubert Epps, arriving to accompany his son to breakfast in the hopes of starting his day off on the right foot.

Myrtle shoved him out of the way to continue to Miles's car, but found that Hubert's car blocked Miles's car so she jumped into Hubert's car instead and locked the doors.

Boone appeared in the doorway, glowering behind the confused Hubert.

"What's going on?" asked Hubert.

Fortunately, Hubert had been short-sighted enough to leave the keys in the ignition. Myrtle started the car and put the window down a hair. In the distance, she could hear the sound of a siren.

"You know *exactly* what's going on, Hubert," said Myrtle coldly. "You've been trying to cover it up for years. Boone killed Tara Blanton and hid her body on your property. And you pushed your wife down the stairs to cover it up because she was determined to get at the truth after all these years. Pearl never stopped feeling sorry for Tara's parents and felt like they deserved the truth."

Hubert leaned his side against his car as if his feet were giving way. "Boone?" he asked weakly. "Not Rose?"

Boone's face was lit up with weird shadows from the headlights and his wide grin was more of a sneer as the siren grew louder. "You always did favor Rose, Daddy. You wouldn't have protected *me*, would you? You'd have picked the phone right up and called Red. And Mama wouldn't have been writing a book, either."

Myrtle said, "Why exactly *did* Pearl choose to reveal the secrets with a book? She and Rose were very close—why didn't Pearl just ask Rose to turn herself in? Convince her that she would have received a lighter sentence and relieved her conscience if she went to the police?"

Hubert said, "Pearl tried. Every time that she or I brought it up, Rose would look as if she was on the verge of collapse. Then she'd burst into tears and either leave the house or hang up the phone. Then she'd be a disaster for days. It was impossible to talk with her about it."

Then Hubert turned on Boone angrily. "As to whether I'd have protected you like I protected Rose? You're right; I wouldn't have. That's because you never needed protecting. You were always tough. Too tough. That's why we're in this mess to begin with. And why *wouldn't* I think Rose had done it? She's the one who fell apart. She's the one who keeps saying that it's all her fault. Rose is the one who became a shadow of herself."

Myrtle said, "Because she was trying to be a good sister and do what Boone said. She felt guilty for not protecting Tara from Boone and for arguing with Tara about something trivial during their last conversation. Boone said they could get away with hiding Tara's body—and they did. For a while."

"Although it was quixotic of me to think so," snarled Boone. Hubert blinked at him.

Myrtle said, "What I'm not sure is when and how you and Pearl found out about Tara. It must have been in the last ten years or so. I simply can't see Pearl keeping a secret for thirty years: not a secret as big and awful as that one, anyway. Was she gardening and came across bones? She always found gardening to be a tremendous escape. How terrible that must have been for her! There she was, planting a bed of bushes and perennials and she found something dark and tragic."

Boone sighed. "Mama should have called before she dug. She was too close to the sewer line to be digging there, anyway. And yes, since Daddy isn't inclined to answer, it was about ten years ago."

Hubert was still staring at Boone. Then he lunged at him, reaching for his throat while Myrtle lay on the horn of Hubert's car. But Boone was lean and fit and easily side-stepped him. Hubert slumped again, still furious, against his car.

"You're not worthy to even say her name," said Hubert, gasping for air.

"Maybe I'm not, but you're *especially* not, seeing as how you killed her," said Boone casually.

The police car was at the dealership now, but fortunately neither man seemed inclined to run. Red, wearing a tee shirt and sweatpants, ran up to them, hand on his weapon. When he saw his mother sitting calmly in Hubert's car, he dropped his hand. "Hubert? Boone? What's going on here, guys?" he asked guardedly.

Boone drawled, "Daddy and I have both confessed to your mama."

Myrtle put the window all the way down. "Not a full confession, Boone. You didn't confess to killing Nell."

Boone gave a snort. "That's right. I suppose I lost track with all the confessing going on."

"I didn't confess to anything," said Hubert sharply.

"That's because I confessed for you. I don't mind getting the blame for Nell and Tara, but I'm sure not taking it for Mama. That's all on you," said Boone, eyes narrowing.

Red was already getting the handcuffs off his belt. "All right, I've heard enough. Let's finish talking about this back at the station. Hands behind your backs." He carefully cuffed Boone and Hubert and guided them into the police car.

"Bye, Miss M!" said Boone cheerfully. "No hard feelings about earlier, right?"

Myrtle rolled her eyes at him and Boone plopped into the backseat of the cruiser.

Red made a quick phone call to Lieutenant Perkins to update him. Then he looked at Myrtle as he rubbed the side of his face. He shook his head. "I'm really not sure what you're doing at dawn at the dealership. And in Hubert's vehicle, to boot. Are you okay?"

"I'm absolutely fine. Neither of them touched a single hair on my head," said Myrtle with a sniff.

Red tilted his head to look at her. "You shouldn't be driving yourself back home, Mama. You've obviously had a really stressful experience."

"I'm *fine*," said Myrtle through gritted teeth.

"I'm going to call Miles and get him to come out here and drive you back," said Red briskly taking out his phone.

"Good luck doing that," said Myrtle, holding Miles's phone up for him to see. "And I have his car, too."

Red blinked at it. "Okay, not sure what you're doing with that. You've got Miles's phone and Miles's and Hubert's cars. Seems like there's a theme of light thievery going on. Never mind, I'll call Elaine and have her come out and drive you back."

"Don't you dare wake little Jack up," said Myrtle hotly. "The very idea! I'll simply drive Miles's car back to my house. For heaven's sake."

Red said, "Fine. And I'll follow you home. Which, considering the speed you ordinarily drive, should take us until the end of the day."

Chapter Twenty-One

Naturally, it did *not* take until the end of the day. Red's hyperbole made Myrtle drive a bit speedier than her usual twenty-five mile-per-hour clip. She drove straight back to her house, without stopping to drop off Miles's phone.

It took Red a little while to process Hubert and Boone's arrests and to speak with the state police when they arrived. While she was waiting, Myrtle ate another hearty breakfast and worked on her crossword puzzle, which she was able to complete in a mere fifteen minutes.

When Red and Lieutenant Perkins from the state police finally showed up, Myrtle was just pouring herself another cup of coffee. After seeing Red's face, she said, "Here, take this one. I'll make myself another. You need it more than I do." She beamed at Perkins. "I'm glad we have the chance to talk again! Can I make you a cup of coffee?"

"Good to see you, Mrs. Clover," said Perkins in his even voice. "And no, I'm fine, thank you."

"You certainly do look better-rested than Red does," observed Myrtle.

Red glowered at her. "Some of us aren't used to getting up before dawn, Mama."

"It *was* dawn. That's why I was going to the car dealership. It wasn't even that early," said Myrtle.

"*Early* is relative," said Red. He took a large sip of the coffee.

Myrtle settled into a chair. "I suppose Hubert and Boone told you everything?" she asked.

Perkins shook his head. "Unfortunately, no. Instead, they asked for lawyers. It remains to be seen what information, if any, they'll provide us. So we'd be very grateful to you if you could share what you know."

Myrtle preened while Red glowered at her.

Red said, "Of course, it's just your word against theirs. Hearsay."

"On the contrary," said Myrtle, looking down her nose at Red. "As a matter of fact, Miles has this nifty app on his phone. It's a voice recorder. While I was in the car, I was able to tape what they said."

Perkins raised his eyebrows. "A full confession?"

Myrtle thought back over the rather tense conversation she'd had with the two men. "I'm afraid not. But there should be enough material there for you to convict them. And I can tell you the rest of it."

Red groaned and Perkins gave him a repressive look. "That would be very helpful, Mrs. Clover."

"Where should I begin? I'll start with poor Tara. Because that's where everything started," said Myrtle. She frowned. "I'm so annoyed with myself for not seeing it decades ago and for trusting our very incompetent police department at the time.

You see, Tara wasn't the type of girl to run away at all. And she didn't—she was right here all along. Red knew a very important piece of information."

Red cocked his eyebrows and Myrtle continued, "Although he didn't realize that he knew it or of its importance. Where my book club friend, Georgia, thought that Boone and Tara were dating, Red knew that Boone and Tara were *not* dating but that Boone *wanted* to date Tara. There's a world of difference between those two things."

Perkins nodded. "Tara didn't want to date Boone."

"That's right. It all came to a head the night of the party, which makes sense—no one was on their best behavior because they'd all been drinking. Inhibitions were lowered. Rose argued with Tara that night, despite the fact that they were the best of friends," said Myrtle.

Perkins looked intently at Myrtle. "So Rose killed Tara."

"No, Boone did. Rose simply argued with her. But Boone, according to him, gave Tara a shove out of frustration. That shove went badly wrong and resulted in Tara knocking her head and dying from her injury," said Myrtle. "You can hear that on Miles's phone."

"Okay," said Red. "Boone tried to persuade Tara once again to be his girlfriend. She rejected him and he pushed her, causing a freak accident and Tara's death. Then they bury the body where the sewer line was being installed. So where does Pearl's death come in?"

Myrtle shot him an annoyed look for rushing her through her spotlight performance. "I was getting to that. Thirty years ago, Pearl and Hubert, totally unsuspecting, come back from their weekend away. They discovered a very different Rose."

Perkins asked, "Boone didn't change?"

Red said, "Boone became even *more* Boone-like, if that makes sense. Boisterous, sometimes-sullen, prone to drinking and partying. But he didn't change like Rose did."

"Rose became a shadow of herself. She was jumpy, cried a lot, and didn't want to leave the house. She gave up her old friends and just stayed with her family. Rose was a mess," said Myrtle.

Perkins asked, "And what did her family make of all this? Is that when they realized that Tara Blanton was buried in their front yard?"

Myrtle shook her head. "No. They probably told themselves that it was a natural reaction to Tara 'running away.' That Rose missed Tara or perhaps felt guilty about her role in helping Tara run away. Then, about ten years ago, Pearl discovered Tara." Myrtle looked at both men. "It's on Miles's phone."

"How did Pearl do that?" asked Perkins.

"One of Pearl's favorite pastimes was gardening. She was working to create a bed at the front of the house and made a terrible discovery. Boone said that his mother shouldn't have been gardening around the sewer lines to begin with, but Pearl carefully planted shallow-rooted butterfly weed, daylilies, and native ornamental grasses. I walked over there last night to see what was there. But she somehow managed to keep that discovery a secret for the next ten years. I have a feeling Hubert persuaded her to do so. He was very protective of Rose—and he and Pearl both apparently thought that Rose had been responsible for Tara's death." Myrtle took a sip of her coffee and watched the men's reaction.

Red said, "Why would they think that? If anybody in their family acted like he might have killed somebody, it would have been Boone. He was the bad boy of the family."

Myrtle shrugged. "But Boone hadn't perceptibly changed. Besides, Boone allowed them to believe that Rose had been involved and Rose was too weak at the time to set the story straight. Or maybe she didn't care to—because Tara was dead and nothing would change that. Plus, Rose felt very guilty over everything that had happened: that she'd had a party, that Tara had been there, that she'd argued with her friend, and that her brother had killed her. She even *said* that it was all her fault."

Perkins thought this over for a minute, nodding. "Pearl and Hubert harbor this terrible secret that ends up damaging their family. They go on as normal, though? No one notices a change in the two of them?"

Myrtle said, "I wasn't surprised when I heard that they'd found out about Tara in the last ten years. That's because both of them *did* change, and rather dramatically."

Red stared at her. "What do you mean? Pearl was still out doing good everywhere she could, and with a big smile on her face, same as always."

"Yes, but she threw herself even more into her charitable acts. She was *fervent*. Obsessed, even. I remember wondering if she was trying to escape Hubert, which is why I didn't really question Pearl about it. That's when Hubert went on his self-destructive mission, remember?" asked Myrtle.

Red frowned. "You mean the drinking? Mama, I have to break it to you—Hubert always drank."

"Not like that," said Myrtle. "He was even drunk at the garden club gala."

Red snorted. "All the ladies are tipsy at the garden club gala. And look at your book club! They were all toasted."

Myrtle glared at him. "This wasn't the same. Hubert *showed up* intoxicated at the garden club gala. Then he drank *more* and had to leave. And if I dropped by the house to see Pearl, he was always drinking."

Perkins asked, "Always drinking . . . in the evening?"

"No, I'm talking about ten a.m.," said Myrtle. "I'm serious—he had a problem. I assumed that his problem was what was driving Pearl out into the world of volunteering. But maybe Pearl was trying to make amends for the fact that a member of her family had taken a life."

"So we have a real change in behavior in the family after Tara is discovered," said Perkins. "Then what? How about Pearl's sister . . . Nell? How did she change when she heard the news?"

Myrtle shook her head. "Nell wasn't originally told. I'm certain of it."

Red said, "Now this we can agree on. I don't see Pearl and Hubert telling Nell, either."

"Why is that?" asked Perkins.

"Because Nell was a virtuous woman. If Pearl had breathed a word of Tara's death to her, she'd have picked up that big pocketbook of hers and stomped right off to the police station to tell them. No, they had to keep it from her. And that's likely another reason why this huge secret started to weigh so heavily on Pearl.

It came between her and her sister," said Myrtle. "Pearl told me as much herself when she was dropping her manuscript by my house."

Perkins said, "So Pearl decided to unburden herself of her secret and share it with the world. She'd have known what would have happened . . . that someone in her family would go to jail."

"In her mind, her family had already gotten a 'get out of jail free' card for decades. She saw the effects that keeping secrets was having on her family—Hubert was drinking too much, Rose's personality completely changed. Boone . . . well, he was just even *more* Boone. She warned them all that she would write a book," said Myrtle. "And then she announced later that she'd finished it. The thing is that the person who was most obviously and immediately upset was Edward Hammond. He ended up storming out."

Red snorted. "He sure got the wrong impression of what the book would be covering."

"Pearl had said it would be a memoir. To Edward, that meant that there wouldn't be a whole lot of material and that it would also cover the lives of those close to Pearl, like her sister. He felt that Nell's reputation needed to be protected. But, despite his strong reaction, someone else that night had an equally-strong reaction—Boone. It just wasn't evident at the time. But the next morning, he made sure to retrieve the laptop from his mother's house when she left. Then he broke into my house after his mother had dropped off the manuscript." Myrtle pressed her lips together in displeasure.

"He didn't really *break in*, considering that all of your windows were open," said Red dryly.

"As an invitation to a *cat*. Not for anyone to just come climbing in my windows," said Myrtle.

Perkins said, "Then he went back to his parents' house and pushed his mother down the stairs. That's pretty cool and collected."

Myrtle shook her head. "I think you'll find that *Hubert* pushed Pearl down the stairs."

"What?" Red and Perkins chimed in together.

Myrtle nodded sagely. "That is correct. You see, Hubert thought he was protecting *Rose* all this time. Pearl thought the same thing, although she'd thought the time for protecting her daughter was over. Hubert argued with his wife about revealing their secret and in a last, desperate attempt to protect Rose, he gave Pearl a shove that ended up taking her life."

Perkins considered this for a few moments. "Boone didn't do it."

"No. As far as Boone was concerned, the problem was solved. He had *stolen* the book and the laptop," said Myrtle.

Red sighed. "But that didn't *really* solve his problem. Pearl could have gone to the police and told us about Tara's death."

"I never said that Boone wasn't shortsighted," said Myrtle with a shrug. "Or perhaps he felt as though he could use his charm and persuade his mother not to go to the cops."

"So Pearl is dead. Why was Nell murdered?" asked Perkins. "It sounds as if she knew absolutely nothing about the secrets in the book."

Red said, "Maybe she saw something that implicated Hubert in Pearl's death."

Myrtle shook her head. "Nell died because Rose finally couldn't take the guilt anymore. She had to unload."

Perkins said, "But why not unload her secrets to her father? Wouldn't that make the most sense? He already knew everything, after all."

"He *thought* he knew. But he didn't. He thought that *Rose* had killed Tara. If he'd known it was Boone, Hubert never would have protected him as he tried to protect Rose. In a way, Rose was trying to protect her brother. Plus, she was angry at her father. I'd witnessed her leaving him at the Goodwill. I think she knew that her father was responsible for her mother's death," said Myrtle.

Perkins put a hand up to rub his temple as if a headache was coming on. "Okay. So Rose goes to tell Nell everything. That Boone had killed Tara and that she was buried in the Epps yard. That Boone had stolen the book with all the secrets. That her father had killed her mother. So what happened to Nell? Did Rose kill her so that she wouldn't go to the police?"

Myrtle shook her head. "No. Rose wouldn't have minded at this point if her aunt had reported the crimes. She wanted that responsibility taken off her hands. No, the problem was that Boone had seen his sister go into his aunt's house. He knew the condition that Rose was in and that she was at a breaking point. He confronted Rose about it angrily and Rose fell apart and admitted that she'd told Nell everything."

Red said, "But 'everything' wasn't good for Boone."

"Exactly. And Nell, as we've established, was not the type to keep secrets. She was likely getting ready to go to the police when Boone walked in and murdered her," said Myrtle.

Perkins said, "And Hubert just found out that Rose *hadn't* murdered Tara?"

"That's right. He found out while we were at the car dealership. Boone told him. Hubert and Pearl were convinced it was Rose because they thought her behavior was due to her guilt. Instead, it was just that Rose was keeping a terrible secret and it absolutely ate her up," said Myrtle.

Red said, "I just can't believe that you went out there to confront Boone, Mama."

Myrtle glared indignantly at him. "I certainly did *not*. I was out at his dealership to find Miles's phone. That's *it*. I only went over to the showroom when I saw him in there. I had no intention of confronting him—I was trying to get away from there before he'd noticed. I'd seen Pearl's laptop, you see. And then all the pieces fell into place."

Perkins said, "Well, you've surely helped us out, Mrs. Clover. With your recording and with what you've just told us, I'm sure we can put Boone and Hubert Epps away for a long time."

He jumped as something rubbed against his leg. Seeing Myrtle's black cat, he reached down and cautiously petted her.

"Darling Pasha," said Myrtle lovingly. "Looking for more food."

Red said, "That reminds me that I have a passel of coupons to give you. Elaine got some in the mail."

"Well, bring them on over later. They're still running the sale at the store. Maybe once you're done with everything at the station today, you can drive me over to the grocery store. Those cans of cat food won't haul themselves, you know. And Miles is apparently too sick to even get out of the bed today," said Myrtle.

With that, there was a polite tap on the door. Red opened it up to Miles.

Miles had made an attempt to look better than he felt. But his hair was askew and he wore track pants and a sweatshirt instead of his usual khakis and button downs. And his eyes were watery and red.

"May I please have my phone?" he asked.

Perkins and Red shook their heads at him. "Afraid that's a negative," said Red.

"What did I miss?" asked Miles.

"Let's walk back to your house and I'll tell you all about it," said Myrtle.

About the Author:

E lizabeth writes the Southern Quilting mysteries and Memphis Barbeque mysteries for Penguin Random House and the Myrtle Clover series for Midnight Ink and independently. She blogs at ElizabethSpannCraig.com/blog, named by Writer's Digest as one of the 101 Best Websites for Writers. Elizabeth makes her home in Matthews, North Carolina, with her husband. She's the mother of two.

Sign up for Elizabeth's free newsletter to stay updated on releases:

https://bit.ly/2xZUXqO

This and That

I love hearing from my readers. You can find me on Facebook as Elizabeth Spann Craig Author, on Twitter as elizabethscraig, on my website at elizabethspanncraig.com, and by email at elizabethspanncraig@gmail.com.

Thanks so much for reading my book...I appreciate it. If you enjoyed the story, would you please leave a short review on the site where you purchased it? Just a few words would be great. Not only do I feel encouraged reading them, but they also help other readers discover my books. Thank you!

Did you know my books are available in print and ebook formats? Most of the Myrtle Clover series is available in audio and some of the Southern Quilting mysteries are. Find the audiobooks here.

Please follow me on BookBub for my reading recommendations and release notifications.

I'd also like to thank some folks who helped me put this book together. Thanks to my cover designer, Karri Klawiter, for her awesome covers. Thanks to my editor, Judy Beatty for her help. Thanks to beta readers Amanda Arrieta and Dan Harris for all of their helpful suggestions and careful reading. Thanks to my ARC readers for helping to spread the word. Thanks, as always, to my family and readers.

Other Works by Elizabeth:

Myrtle Clover Series in Order (be sure to look for the Myrtle series in audio, ebook, and print):

Pretty is as Pretty Dies

Progressive Dinner Deadly

A Dyeing Shame

A Body in the Backyard

Death at a Drop-In

A Body at Book Club

Death Pays a Visit

A Body at Bunco

Murder on Opening Night

Cruising for Murder

Cooking is Murder

A Body in the Trunk

Cleaning is Murder

Edit to Death

Hushed Up

A Body in the Attic

Murder on the Ballot

Death of a Suitor (2021)

Southern Quilting Mysteries in Order:
Quilt or Innocence
Knot What it Seams
Quilt Trip
Shear Trouble
Tying the Knot
Patch of Trouble
Fall to Pieces
Rest in Pieces
On Pins and Needles
Fit to be Tied
Embroidering the Truth
Knot a Clue
Quilt-Ridden (2021)

The Village Library Mysteries in Order (Debuting 2019):
Checked Out
Overdue
Borrowed Time
Hush-Hush
Where There's a Will (2021)

Memphis Barbeque Mysteries in Order (Written as Riley Adams):
Delicious and Suspicious
Finger Lickin' Dead
Hickory Smoked Homicide
Rubbed Out

And a standalone "cozy zombie" novel: Race to Refuge, written as Liz Craig